LEVIATHAN'S WAKE

ATTICUS BLACKWOOD

PROLOGUE

In the depths of the northern Pacific Ocean, within an advanced underwater research station, a dedicated scientist sits at his desk, carefully scrutinizing the details of the government funding they have received. His eyes are fixed on the screen, absorbing every line of text with intense focus. This ambitious project holds the potential to revolutionize the world as we know it, and he is acutely aware of the magnitude of its importance. There is no room for error; the stakes are high, and the success of this endeavor is paramount.

The scientist's intense focus was abruptly interrupted by a sudden knock at the door. "Come in," he called out, and his research assistant entered, informing him that the test was already in progress. Quickly shutting down his computer, the scientist urged his assistant to hurry, emphasizing the importance of not missing the excitement. As they made their way down the seemingly endless hallway, the assistant couldn't help but voice her uncertainty. "Do you truly believe that we can clone a dinosaur from the DNA we discovered on the ocean floor?" she asked. With unwavering determination, the scientist responded, "We've dedicated years to studying how to revive dinosaurs. Today marks the moment when we bring a dinosaur back to the world of the living."

"I was surprised to find Plesiosaurus DNA in the Pacific," the assistant exclaimed. "But I shouldn't have been. The ocean is the perfect place to find viable DNA. When we tried using bones, they were too dry and barely had any trace left." Before the assistant could finish speaking, the entire base began to shake. The hallway turned a foreboding shade of red as alarms blared around them. They exchanged a worried glance before sprinting down the hallway.

The ground trembled once more, causing her to lose her balance and fall to the ground. The scientist tried to assist her, but he, too, was knocked down as the base shuddered again. As he looked up to inquire about the situation, his words were drowned out by the eerie hissing and crackling sounds that filled the air, resembling a snake's ominous hiss. Before he could address his assistant, the walls ruptured, and water gushed into the hallway, engulfing them. As he began to lose consciousness, he caught sight of two piercing red lights, almost resembling menacing eyes, fixated on him.

ACT 1

THE CALM BEFORE THE STORM

1

The gentle patter of rain against the window roused Thomas from his slumber before his alarm had a chance to. Glancing at his phone, he saw the time - 4:15 am. Although his day was due to commence in a mere 15 minutes, he yearned for a few more moments of rest. Turning, he gazed upon his wife, Mary, who was still peacefully asleep. Her velvety dark skin and luscious curls filled him with wonder, and he marveled at how he had been blessed with such breathtaking beauty as his partner. As he rose and slipped out of bed, he made his way to the bathroom.

Thomas flicked on the switch, flooding the bathroom with light. His reflections stared back at him from the mirror, framed by his unruly black hair and complemented by his deep brown skin. The stark contrast between his appearance and the pristine whiteness of the bathroom struck him. As he met his own gaze, he felt the weight of exhaustion and apprehension for the journey ahead. The steady flow of water from the tap filled the silence as he began to brush his teeth. Suddenly, a noise at the door drew his attention. Mary, clad in silk pajamas, stood there with a radiant smile and a sparkle in her eyes.

"Thomas, why are we starting so early? The sun isn't even up yet," Mary inquired. Thomas paused in the middle of brushing his teeth and replied, "James wants to meet early. It was his idea, but I'd rather stay in bed with you." Exiting the bathroom, Thomas proceeded to change into his everyday attire while Mary observed. "So, what's the plan for this year?" she asked. After putting on his shirt and grabbing his jacket, Thomas explained, "The plan is to catch as much fish as possible and make a lot of money, just like every year." Curious, Mary asked what else was part of the plan. As he was about to head downstairs, Thomas stopped, turned to his wife, and said, "Well, of course, to come back safe to my beautiful wife." She smiled and gave him a goodbye kiss as he walked out the front door and headed down the steps.

2

As Thomas stepped out of the front door, a blast of cold air hit him, sending a shiver down his spine. He began his journey up the street, the frigid morning air stinging his cheeks. He couldn't help but question his decision not to take his car. However, perhaps he needed the biting wind to jolt him awake. The icy gusts served as a necessary wake-up call, rousing him from his slumber.

He ventured out of the residential neighborhood and found himself on the outskirts of Kodiak Point, a quaint Alaskan town. This place was his only haven, the very foundation of his existence. Growing up here, he witnessed the town's gradual transformation, observing his father's voyages and eventually joining him as a crew member. Today, he commands the same vessel that once belonged to his father.

As Thomas strolled through the quiet downtown area, he passed by rows of shuttered shops, their windows reflecting the early morning light. The deserted streets were an unusual sight, except for one solitary establishment. He often pondered why James was so keen on starting his day at such an early hour, a habit he shared with Thomas's father. Finally, Thomas arrived at the Kodiak Bar & Grill, the sole place open at this ungodly hour. The modest brick building held a treasure trove of memories, particularly of his father delivering rousing speeches to the crew before embarking on their voyages. Just as he reached for the door, it swung open abruptly, catching him off guard.

Before him stood the stunned figure of Nora Anderson, her wide brown eyes resembling a deer caught in headlights, prompting Thomas to chuckle. As the door closed behind her, Nora apologized, explaining that she had just dropped off her father before her shift and hoped she hadn't startled him. Thomas reassured her and remarked, "So James is already inside. I was hoping to beat him here, but your old man is always early." Nora smiled and replied, "I have to get to the hospital early to prepare for the arrival of the sailors." Thomas looked puzzled and asked why she needed to prepare. Nora returned his gaze with a knowing look and explained, "Just because your crew returns safely and unharmed doesn't mean everyone will." Thomas smirked and retorted that the other captains needed to do a better job. "Don't say that; luckily, it's only us out here. You know the other captains already don't like you," Nora cautioned. Thomas bid her farewell with a hug and headed inside the bar, mindful not to keep her dad waiting.

3

Thomas entered the cozy bar, immediately feeling the warmth envelop him. To his right, he noticed several empty seats scattered across the middle of the floor and unoccupied booths lining the wall. Turning his gaze to the left, he spotted Nancy behind the bar, her vibrant red hair tied up in a bun as she meticulously cleaned a glass. Approaching her, he greeted her and was met with a pair of striking bright green eyes. "Oh, Thomas, you're here too. I thought it was going to be a quiet morning," Nancy remarked. Thomas glanced around and observed the lack of other customers. "Well, with you and James here, I suppose I'll need to brew more coffee, or perhaps you'd prefer something stronger?" she suggested. Thomas smiled and politely declined, opting for a cup of coffee instead.

I heard a stern voice coming from behind the counter. "Nancy, what did I tell you about getting the sailors drunk this early in the morning?" The voice belonged to Brian, the owner of the bar. He was a slender man with a bald head and a kind demeanor towards all the sailors. Brian always made sure that everyone felt welcome, especially during the busy season. His care for the sailors had a lasting impact on me as I grew up. Despite the number of sailors leaving town during the off-season, Brian always made sure they felt at home when they returned.

I called out to Brian, asking what he was doing down there. He explained that the bar hose was leaking and needed to be fixed before the place filled up with hungry, intoxicated sailors. I chuckled and inquired about James. Nancy pointed to the back of the bar, where I spotted a large, weathered man with a bald head, a salt-and-pepper beard, and a welcoming smile. I thanked her and made my way over to James's booth.

Thomas took a seat opposite James and greeted him. James engrossed himself in the morning paper and, with a notebook by his coffee, raised a finger to signal Thomas to wait. After a minute, Nancy brought Thomas his coffee, and James finally set down the paper. "I was just reading about the mayor's plans to expand the port for larger ships," James remarked. Irritated, Thomas tossed the paper onto his seat. "The mayor's affairs are of no concern to me. Do you have the crew list for this year?" he inquired.

James gave Thomas a stern look and opened his notebook. "I do, but first, have you charted a course for the upcoming season?" Thomas leaned back in his seat and replied, "It's nearly complete, but I still require last year's weather reports and need to speak with Philip as well." James maintained his unwavering gaze on Thomas as he tried to avoid eye contact. "Make sure it's done before we set sail, and it should be fine," James said. "I have the crew list and everyone's roles; let me know if you have any objections," he added, and Thomas instructed James to proceed.

"Alright, it looks like we have almost the entire crew from last year coming back, which is not surprising, along with the two new recruits you select-ed. First, there's Willam Carter, our ship engineer. The last time I spoke with him, he seemed eager to set sail. Then there's Daniel King, our bait mas-ter, who has a confidence that matches the size of the ship. He may be cocky, but he's good at what he does. Follow-ing them, we have Matthew Lewis and Andrew Quinn, who handle process-ing the fish. Andrew is quite pleased that you brought Matthew on board; he really helped with the extra work-load we had last time. Next on the ros-ter is Joshua Robinson, our radio op-erator. Despite his talkative nature, he's a great fit for the role. Then we have the cook, who happens to be your father's favorite, Chris Johnson. I'm hoping he expands his menu beyond just soup this year. Our deckhands will be Michael Brown, Richard Even, Joseph Foster, Charlie Green, Paul Owens, and finally, Steven Perez. I really like this group of deckhands; they always manage to have a good time, even when they're covered in fish guts. Lastly, we have your two newcomers, Anthoney Miller and David Davis. I haven't had the chance to meet them yet, but I believe they checked in at the lodge yesterday. Is there anyone in this lineup that you anticipate having issues with?" James inquired.

After finishing his drink, Thomas said, "I have no problem with that. I need you to locate all of them and inform them that we are embarking on Monday. However, we will gather here on Sunday at 12 pm in the backroom to discuss the voyage. I will take care of the final preparations before we depart." James nodded and replied, "Will do, captain." Standing up, he added, "I'll see you on Friday," bid farewell, and left the bar. Thomas remained seated, gazing out the window as the rain subsided and the snow continued to fall.

4

As James stepped out of the dimly lit bar, he reached for his notepad and meticulously jotted down the names of the crew. With the morning sun just beginning to ascend at 6:45 am, he made the decision to head back to Fisherman Row. As he stowed away his notepad, he set off on his journey, intending to visit William Carter first, knowing he would likely be at home.

James trudged through the thick blanket of snow, regretting his decision to catch a ride with his daughter instead of driving himself. As he passed by rows of houses, he made his way to the imposing William Carter house. James had known William for years, having sailed for Thomas's father and now for Thomas himself. William always had faith in Thomas, predicting that he would become a great captain. James finally arrived at the two-story red brick house and ascended the steps to knock on the door. The door swung open, revealing William, a large, jovial black man with a substantial belly. At 39, this would mark William's third season sailing under Thomas. "Well, well, if it isn't James Anderson. If you're here, then it's time to set sail," William boomed. "I could be here just to say hello, you know," James replied, to which William burst into laughter. "You're not the type to make those kinds of visits. When are we leaving?" William inquired. James smirked and informed him that they would be leaving on Monday, but they would meet at the Kodiak Bar & Grill on Sunday at 12 pm. William grinned and said, "I'll see you there." After bidding each other goodbye, William closed the door, and James took out his notepad to cross off William's name.

James strolled purposefully toward the doorstep of Michael Brown's house. He had first met Michael three years ago when Thomas had brought him onto the team. Michael was a young man with a newborn baby. James never delved into Michael's personal life, as Michael preferred to keep that to himself, and James respected his privacy. All James knew was that Michael was a hard worker and a valuable addition to the crew. As James knocked on the door, a tall man with a buzz cut and brown skin, holding a baby, answered. "Hey, Mr. Anderson, how are you?" Michael greeted, looking like he hadn't slept all night. "I told you to just call me James. It looks like your newborn is keeping you busy," James responded. Michael adjusted the baby in his arms and replied, "Yeah, he likes to cry a lot, but I still love him all the same. Is something up?" James glanced at Michael's son and smiled as memories of his own daughters flooded his mind. "Yes, I wanted to tell you that we are setting sail on Monday, but we will meet at Kodiak Bar & Grill at 12 pm on Sunday," James said. Michael nodded his understanding and expressed his gratitude. James bid farewell to Michael and his son, then continued down the sidewalk. He took out his notepad and crossed off Michael's name.

James strolled past several houses until he spotted Richard Even tinkering with his 1991 Mustang in the driveway. It had been six years since James had first met Richard, just before Thomas's father retired. Richard was a no-nonsense man known for commanding respect. However, after losing his wife the previous year, James didn't know if Richard still had the desire to sail. It had been a tough time, but the crew had rallied around him. Now, it was just Richard and his sixteen-year-old daughter. Despite his compact frame, Richard still had a formidable presence. He was short, stocky, with a bald head and dark skin, and was as strong as an ox.

As James approached, Richard finally noticed him and set down his wrench. "Hello, James. I suppose it's that time, isn't it?" Richard said. James smiled and replied, "That's if you still want to go. I would understand if you need more time." Richard shook his head and said, "I need the money, and some time at sea would do me good. Besides, my daughter is visiting her aunt, and I'll be here alone." James nodded in approval and said that they would set sail on Monday, with a plan to meet at the Kodiak Bar & Grill on Sunday at 12 pm. Richard shook his hand and confirmed he would be there. As Richard went back to working on his car, James walked away, pulling out his notepad and crossing off Richard's name.

James made his way down to Charlie Green's quaint house. Charlie, a wise and reserved black man, had crossed paths with James two years prior when Thomas assumed the role of captain. Despite his quiet demeanor, Charlie had a deep passion for fishing, evident in the sparkle that lit up his eyes whenever a fresh catch was brought on board. As James approached the porch, he spotted Charlie and his wife engrossed in their respective books. With a friendly wave, James announced from the sidewalk, "We'll be setting sail on Monday, but let's meet on Sunday at 12 pm at the Kodiak Bar & Grill." Charlie, without looking up from his book, simply flashed a thumbs up in acknowledgment. Although Charlie's wife remained immersed in her reading, James could discern a smile on her face, knowing her husband was about to embark on another seafaring adventure. With a content smile, James mentally checked off Charlie's name from his list. "If only more people were like Charlie," James mused to himself, "the world would be a much simpler place." With that thought, he continued on his leisurely walk, savoring the tranquility of the neighborhood.

James arrived at Steven Perez's house and was about to knock on the door when it swung open. Standing there was a short, curly-haired young man holding a milk bottle. He explained that he had seen James approaching and wanted to make sure the baby was settled before answering the door. Steven mentioned that it had taken him five hours to get the baby to sleep. James reassured him and then informed Steven that they would set sail on Monday, but they should meet at the Kodiak Bar & Grill on Sunday at 12 pm. Steven agreed and closed the door quietly so as not to wake the baby. Chuckling to himself, James reflected on the challenges of getting his own children to sleep when they were babies. He then took out his notepad and crossed off Steven's name.

James didn't have to travel far as Andrew Quinn lived right next door. James strolled over and rapped on the door, anticipating a towering, blond Viking-like man to greet him. However, to his surprise, a petite, fair-skinned girl with short blonde hair, sipping on a glass of milk, opened the door. "Hello Nora, is your father home?" James inquired, and she nodded before calling out for her father. Moments later, the man he was expecting emerged at the door. Andrew instructed his daughter to wait inside, and she bid James goodbye as he reciprocated the gesture. "So, what's the plan, James?" Andrew inquired. "We're setting sail on Monday, but we'll meet at Kodiak Bar & Grill on Sunday at 12 pm," James informed him. Andrew smiled and asked about Thomas. "He's doing well; nothing seems to faze that boy," James replied. However, Andrew's expression betrayed a hint of concern as he remarked, "Yes, but the pressure from the other captain can't be easy on him." James raised his hand and reassured him, "That boy is mentally stronger than all of us. He knows what to focus on and what to ignore." Andrew smiled, closed his eyes, and chuckled softly, saying, "Tell Thomas I'm looking forward to sailing with him again." James nodded and bid Andrew farewell. Andrew retreated into his house, and James proceeded to his next destination, crossing Andrew's name off his list before he left.

James glanced at his watch and noted that it was 9:45 am. Aware that most of the crew members would likely be in town by now, he realized he had one more house to visit before returning. Making his way back to the top of Fisherman's Row, he stopped at a familiar house that held sentimental value - it used to be his before he and his wife relocated further down the street. Approaching the one-story cottage-style house, he knocked on the door and was greeted by his daughter Layla, with her tall, braided hair and warm brown skin. She embraced him, asking how he was doing. "I'm fine, Layla, but I actually came here for Paul," James replied as she pulled away. "Okay, but be nice," she cautioned before calling for Paul to come to the door.

As he waited, James heard the approaching footsteps of his son-in-law. Paul, just as tall as James but smaller in overall body weight, appeared nervous, sweat trickling down his dark-skinned brow. "Hello, Mr. Anderson, how can I help?" Paul asked, but James maintained a stern look on his face. "I told you to call me James, but Thomas has decided we will set sail on Monday, and we will all meet on Sunday at Kodiak Bar & Grill at 12 pm," James informed him. Paul nodded and agreed to be there. When James reached out his hand, Paul reciprocated by shaking it. James's grip was strong, causing Paul to wince slightly before letting go. Layla shot her father a disapproving look, but James just smiled back. He bid them both goodbye and continued up the street.

James gazed across the snow-covered Fisherman's Row, feeling the weight of his responsibility as he looked at the crossed out names on his list. He couldn't help but wish he had driven instead of facing the long walk ahead. Despite the falling snow, passing cars honked and greeted him as they headed into town. Looking down the hill toward the town, he urged himself to keep moving. Determined, he set off toward Neptune's Net Seafood Grill, knowing it was where most of the crew would be at this early hour.

✦

5

As James strolled along the street, he came upon Neptune's Net Seafood Grill, a striking blue establishment adorned with fishing nets hanging from the roof and a trident suspended above the sturdy wooden door. This renowned restaurant was frequented by sailors and offered not only a variety of seafood but also a hearty breakfast. During the off-season, James and his crew could often be found here, relishing a substantial morning meal. Reflecting on the past, James remembered when the restaurant was simply a humble shack serving only fish and chips. Its remarkable transformation over the past three decades was attributed to the owner's daughter, who had elevated it to its current status. As he grasped the door handle and pushed it open, the boisterous cheers of his crew greeted him.

James grinned as he observed his crew occupying the largest table in the restaurant, surrounded by a spread of delicious food. To his left, Joseph Foster, a lively red-headed man, chuckled with a mouthful of bacon. Beside him, Daniel King, our confident baitmaster, sipped coffee from a dainty cup that emphasized his large, dark hands. Across from him, the handsome blonde, Matthew Lewis, scrutinized his steak and eggs for doneness. Then there was Mark Nelson, whose ample belly and gray beard gave him a resemblance to a black Santa Claus, at least in James's eyes. Lastly, Joshua Robinson, a jovial, afro-haired man, couldn't resist cracking jokes. Joshua rose and strode over to James, urging everyone to cheer for their esteemed first mate. The enthusiastic cheers and table-pounding drew the ire of someone in the distant rear of the restaurant, who shouted at them to quiet down.

They all stood frozen in fear as they glanced towards the back of the restaurant and spotted Aubery Walker. Her pale skin and black hair were illuminated by the light as she sat reading the morning paper, emanating an aura of quiet intensity. When James raised his hand to apologize on behalf of his crew, Aubery remained expressionless, returning to her newspaper without a word. After the crew all apologized and James reassured them, he delivered the message that they were to set sail on Monday, with a meeting scheduled at the Kodiak Bar and Grill on Sunday at

12 pm. Joshua, attempting to lighten the mood, joked about not being allowed to meet here after their outburst, but James silenced him with a stern look. The rest of the crew took note of James's warning and fell silent.

"Now, I hope you all remember that you are part of my crew, and you represent me and your captain. I need to start seeing all of you behaving more like adults than children when we set out to sea," James emphasized, his expression serious as the crew exchanged worried glances. "Don't worry, James. We will be on our best behavior. I'll personally ensure it," Mark assured. James glanced around the table and stated, "I'll see you all on Sunday." As James waved back at Aubrey Walker, apologizing once again for his crew, he made his way out the door.

After leaving the building, James pulled out his notepad and carefully crossed off a few more names. Glancing at his watch, he noted that it was now 11:15 am, realizing that the market would be open and there was a chance of finding Chris Johnson there. James then tucked his notepad back into his pocket and, after checking both directions, crossed the street to head towards Captain Catch Market.

6

James strolled through the bustling town until he reached the pier. There, he paused in front of an arch adorned with a large sign reading "Captain Catch Market." This bustling market was a haven for fresh produce, meats, and seafood, offering a wide array of ingredients for a delicious home-cooked meal. James was well aware that every morning, Chris Johnson could be found here, perusing the latest arrivals and seeking out the finest goods available.

As James continued on his search for Chris, he greeted the locals and asked if they had seen him. Some people replied in the negative, while others mentioned seeing Chris at various vendor booths. It seemed that Chris was making the rounds. Undeterred, James kept walking, confident that he would eventually find his friend. Suddenly, as he turned a corner, he spotted a tall, black man with a salt-and-pepper beard similar to his own. However, unlike James, Chris had a full head of hair. James always found it remarkable that they were the same age and couldn't help but touch his bald head whenever he saw Chris.

Chris was in the middle of a heated discussion with a fish vendor when James intervened. "You can't possibly be selling this tiny salmon for that price; it's barely the size of my own leg," Chris exclaimed. Unfazed, the vendor retorted, "If you don't like it, then go somewhere else." Just as Chris was about to continue, James placed a calming hand on his shoulder and urged him to relax. "Oh, hey, James, sorry, but this guy is trying to rip off his customers," Chris said, still glaring at the fish vendor. Just as tensions were reaching a breaking point, James stepped in, diffusing the situation and apologizing for Chris's actions. He then gently guided Chris away from the vendor.

"You can't resist an argument, can you?" James remarked. Chris, with a smile, replied, "You know me, James, I'm never changing. What brings you down here anyway? Are you getting something for you and the wife for dinner?" James covered his face with his hand, let out a deep sigh, and said, "No, I came to inform you that we are setting sail on Monday. We'll meet at Kodiak Bar and Grill on Sunday at 12 pm." Chris patted James on the back and exclaimed, "Perfect!" "Before we leave, I need the entire crew's food allergies and how long we'll be out at sea before returning to port," Chris inquired. James raised his hand and said, "I have the list right here, and we'll be spending three weeks at a time, just like last year." James pulled out a sheet of paper from his pocket and handed it to Chris. After scanning the sheet, Chris remarked, "Oh, this is simple. I'll prepare something that everyone will love. By the way, how is Thomas doing? It's his third season, and he hasn't really connected with the other captains." James shook his head and said, "Since Thomas took over, we've had two of the best seasons our crew has ever had. Thomas will be fine; I have full faith in him." Chris patted James on the back again and said, "Well, if Thomas is fine, then I won't worry. How many greenhorns do we have this year?" James held up two fingers. "I'm heading over to the lodge now to meet them. I got a message saying they checked in last night," James said.

"Shall we expect you and your wife for dinner tonight?" Chris inquired as James began to walk away, flashing a smile. "We wouldn't miss it," James replied. They bid each other goodbye and went their separate ways. Exiting Captain Catch Market, James checked off Chris's name on his notepad. Feeling the strain in his knee from a morning of walking, James sought respite on a bench overlooking the ocean. Reflecting on his age, he pondered whether he had one more season left in him before retiring. Dismissing the thought, he reassured himself that he wasn't old yet. Rising from the bench, James resumed his journey towards Kodiak Point Lodging.

7

As James savored the crisp air during his final stop of the day, he observed the snowfall coming to an end and the sun gradually emerging. He couldn't help but notice the imminent arrival of a new season. However, with the new season came the responsibility of leading two inexperienced crew members who were unfamiliar with our operations. While James hadn't initially chosen to onboard new team members, he trusted Thomas's judgment. Without Thomas's decision to enlist another fish processor, the team wouldn't have been able to manage the substantial amount of fish being brought in.

As he returned to the present, he shook off his wandering thoughts and found himself standing before a sturdy six-story building with a warm tan facade accented by rich brown trim. A prominent sign reading "Kodiak Point Lodging" caught his eye. James observed the bustling scene outside, with numerous sailors coming and going, the staff unloading taxis, and managers scrambling to organize the influx of new guests. It was the time of year when people from out of state would start arriving, eager to settle in before the season began. Amidst the crowd, James recognized familiar faces and greeted them with a wave as he ascended the steps and entered the building.

The interior was a stark contrast to the chaos outside. James appreciated the tranquility of the lobby, where it was evident that security knew how to maintain order among the guests. Making his way to the front desk, he spotted Lily Nelson, a young blonde woman whom he remembered playing with his daughters in the front yard. "Hello, Lily. How are you today?" James inquired. Lily glanced up from her computer, appearing lost in thought, but her face instantly brightened with a huge smile upon seeing James. "Mr. Anderson, I didn't expect you to arrive so soon. Your guests just checked in yesterday," Lily remarked. Just as James was about to respond, a familiar voice behind him interjected, "That's because James has a habit of showing up earlier than expected." James turned to find his good friend Chole Taylor, a tall, slender woman with long grey hair that provided a stark contrast against her fair complexion. "Hello, Chole. I had a feeling I might run into you," James greeted her. Chole approached James and embraced him, inquiring about his wife and mentioning her absence at their recent brunch date. James raised his hand in resignation, admitting that he struggled to keep up with his wife. "You never could, James, but that's alright. I assume you're here about those two newcomers who checked in yesterday," Chole remarked, to which James nodded and confirmed, "Yes, are they still here?" Chole glanced at Lily and discreetly mouthed the word "keys." Lily rummaged through her desk and produced two key cards. "These are their rooms, and as far as I know, they should still be there. I haven't seen them leave their rooms since they checked in," Chole informed James. Lily handed James the key cards and asked if he thought they would last. After thanking her, James accepted the keys and replied, "We'll see," before walking away.

James rode the elevator to the third floor and made his way to room 316. Standing in front of the door, he knocked and waited for David Davis to answer. A voice called out, "I'm coming," prompting James to take a step back so that David could see him through the peephole. As the door unlocked and opened, James found himself face to face with a pale young man with black hair who appeared to be in his twenties.

"I'm assuming you're David Davis," James said with a friendly smile. David nodded and replied, "Yes, I'm David. Thomas mentioned you'd be stopping by. It's a pleasure to meet you, sir. I'm eager to start working with you." James warmly shook David's hand and inquired about his sailing experience. "I've sailed in Florida, but nothing quite like this," David responded. James nodded understandingly and reassured him, "No worries, I've trained people with less experience. Just follow my lead, and we'll be fine." David expressed his gratitude and asked if there was anything else. "Yes, we're setting sail on Monday, but first, we'll meet at the Kodiak Bar and Grill to discuss the upcoming season. Here's a list of all the supplies you'll need to bring, and this gift card has enough funds to cover your expenses. Our captain believes in ensuring everyone is well-prepared." As James handed over the list and the gift card, David was visibly surprised and grateful. "This is beyond what I expected. Thank you so much," David said. James waved off his thanks and bid his goodbyes before David returned to his room.

James made his way to room 330 and rapped on the door, anticipating Anthoney Miller's response. When there was no answer, he knocked again, but to no avail. Frustrated, James pounded on the door, and he could hear the sound of a toilet flushing in the background. Stepping back, he waited as a slightly overweight, sweaty man, who happened to be African American, finally answered the door. James inquired, "Are you, Anthoney Miller?" The man, still looking bewildered, replied, "Yes, I am. Is everything alright? I was in the bathroom when you started banging on the door." James offered a smile and an apology. "I'm James Anderson, the First Mate and Deck Crew Leader. Thomas may have informed you that I would be stopping by." Anthony's face turned red as he said, "Yes, of course, sir. I'm sorry. How can I assist you?" James provided him with the same information and handed Anthoney the same list and gift card that he had given to David. "Thank you, sir. I'm planning to relocate here, and this opportunity will really help me get on my feet." James reassured Anthoney to simply follow his lead and that he would make it back to start his fresh journey. James bid him farewell and began to make his way out of the lodge.

James stood outside the lodge, a notepad in hand, and carefully crossed off the final two names. The sun beamed down, casting its warm glow on his face. As he prepared to head home, the sound of his knees clicking caught his attention. Turning, he spotted a bench overlooking the city and decided to take a seat and make a phone call. "Hello, honey. It seems I've overexerted myself today. Could you possibly come and pick me up?" James asked his wife. She assured him she would be on her way. After ending the call, James settled back on the bench, taking in the picturesque view of his town. His gaze wandered to the ocean, finding solace in the rhythmic movement of the waves as he patiently awaited his wife's arrival.

8

Thomas savored the final sip of his steaming coffee, leaving a generous five-dollar tip on the table as he prepared to depart. Despite the early hour, he knew that the individuals he intended to meet would already be up and about. As he gazed towards the hill leading to the Kodiak Point Lighthouse, his mind wandered to the upcoming visit. His first stop would be the weather station, situated halfway up the hill before reaching the lighthouse.

The snow was beginning to melt slowly, making the ground still quite challenging to navigate. Walking always helped clear his mind of unnecessary thoughts. Although the base of the hill was covered in snow, the path up the hill was clear enough for him to traverse. Thomas hoped for the sun to emerge soon and melt away some of the snow, but it seemed like it would be hours before that happened.

Without complaining, Thomas forged ahead and began the ascent up the hill. The journey wasn't particularly lengthy, but it was strenuous enough to make Thomas break a sweat. Nevertheless, he reached his intended destination—a modest building adorned with radars and satellites on its roof. Approaching the front door, Thomas rapped on it, hoping to catch Ralph's attention through the security cameras. After a prolonged pause, the door clicked open, granting Thomas access inside.

Thomas found himself standing in front of a slender, red-haired man with a beaming smile. The man was sitting in front of an array of five monitors, each displaying different information. "Well, I wasn't expecting you to come by. What can I do for you, Thomas?"

the man named Ralph asked. Thomas, still trying to make sense of the multitude of images on the screens, replied, "Hey Ralph, sorry to bother you so early, but I was hoping to obtain a copy of last year's weather data." Ralph wheeled his chair over to the computer and inquired if Thomas was preparing for the upcoming season. "Yes, I have most things sorted out, but I still like to review the past weather to help me prepare," Thomas explained. As he spoke, the printer in the corner whirred to life, spewing out pages of data. "You've mentioned before that you wish you could conduct field research yourself, but you're needed here," Thomas remarked. Ralph's eyes lit up as he handed Thomas the data, and he eagerly asked, "Do you mean it?" With a smile, Thomas made his way to the door. Before leaving, he promised, "Just wait. Before the season is over, I'll take you out to the sea you research so much." Ralph jumped out of his seat, filled with gratitude, as Thomas closed the door behind him.

9

Thomas gazed out at the weather station, carefully examining the data just handed to him by his friend Ralph. As he studied the intricate charts, he felt deeply grateful for Ralph. Since their childhood, Ralph had been captivated by weather phenomena, and Thomas was thrilled that his friend had secured this position. Having a friend who could provide him with crucial data was invaluable. Glancing up the hill, he spotted the majestic lighthouse. Before returning to town, Thomas knew there was one more person he needed to visit atop that hill.

Thomas continued his journey up the hill, drawing nearer to the lighthouse. As he approached, he caught sight of the figure he had been seeking: Philip Foster, the lighthouse keeper. Philip stood gazing out over the sea, lost in contemplation. Upon hearing Thomas's call, Philip turned around, squinting to discern who was summoning him.

"Hey, Mr. Foster, it's me, Thomas. How are you?" Thomas called out enthusiastically. Philip greeted him with a warm grin and a wave, inviting him to join. "Thomas, I never thought I would see you here this early," Philip remarked. As Thomas approached Philip, the two stood together, gazing out over the sea. Philip, a foot shorter and much older than Thomas, had a head and face covered in grey hair, obscuring many of his facial features. His weathered, dark hands bore the marks of many years spent operating the lighthouse.

"James insisted on meeting early to discuss the upcoming season," Thomas mentioned. Philip gazed at the ocean before reminiscing, "I still recall the days when you were just a little kid, perched on your father's shoulders, seeking my advice for the upcoming season. And now, here you are, a grown man, married to an extraordinary woman and leading the ship your father and James founded. Time really does fly."

Thomas gazed over the town, a smile tugging at the corners of his mouth as memories flooded his mind. "It's become a tradition to seek your insights, and they've never failed us. What do you see out there, Mr. Foster?" Thomas inquired, but Philip's expression betrayed his unease. Concern etched his features as he remarked, "The winds,

.. they're different. There's an unusual force behind them for this time of year. Stand and feel it on your face. Tell me you don't sense it, too." As Thomas complied, a sense of disquiet settled in his eyes. "I do feel it, Mr. Foster. Should I be worried?" he asked while Philip's gaze remained fixed on the ocean. "You must always be concerned, Thomas. The sea is unforgiving. By the way, how is your father faring now that he's retired?" Philip inquired. Unsure of how to interpret this warning, Thomas responded, "He and my mom are enjoying themselves in Hawaii. The only way I see them returning to Kodiak is if Mary and I finally have kids." Philip chuckled, expressing his relief at hearing about Thomas's father's well-being.

"I regret that I can't stay longer, Mr. Foster, but I must head to the Marina," Thomas expressed. Philip finally tore his gaze away from the ocean and turned to face Thomas. Looking up at him, Philip cautioned, "Thomas, take care and always stay vigilant. I know you're an excellent captain, but you must be prepared for anything. Don't underestimate the power of the wind when you're out at sea." Taking in Philip's words, Thomas nodded in understanding. Philip placed his hand on Thomas' shoulder and offered him one final smile before returning his attention to the sea.

As Thomas bid his farewells and began his descent down the hill, he couldn't help but dwell on Philip's words. The unusual behavior of the winds lingered in his mind, especially considering Ralph's data. Comparing last year's wind patterns to the current ones, it was evident that the winds were significantly stronger now.

10

As Thomas strolled through the bustling town, he exchanged friendly waves with familiar faces and engaged in conversations about the upcoming season. Being a lifelong resident, he was well-known to everyone, and the sense of community brought warmth to his heart. Despite the comforting familiarity, he remained focused on his responsibilities. "As the captain, it's my duty to ensure the safety of my crew and bring them back home," he reminded himself. This meant meticulously checking the ship's readiness and safety for the upcoming voyage. Additionally, he reluctantly acknowledged the administrative side of his role and knew that visiting the harbor master's office was essential, even if he didn't particularly enjoy the paperwork. Fortunately, he had taken care of everything well in advance, submitting all required documents a month ahead of schedule.

As he approached the marina, the cacophony of dock workers shouting and sailors scurrying to tend to their boats filled the air. The docks were lined with an assortment of vessels, ranging from commercial ships to those owned by small businesses. Despite the hustle and bustle, Thomas remained unperturbed as he strode past his colleagues. He took pride in his proactive approach, ensuring that his crew could set sail at a moment's notice, although he preferred allowing ample time for preparations. Today, Harborview Marina was particularly bustling, with numerous ships gearing up to embark on their journeys.

Thomas continued on his path and spotted someone he recognized right away. It was Frank Lee, a towering Asian man with a massive black beard that matched his impressive height. "Hello, Frank, how's it going?" Thomas greeted him. Looking down, Frank spotted Thomas and swept him up in a big bear hug. "Oh, my boy, look at you still growing, I see," Frank exclaimed as he set Thomas back on the ground. As Thomas tried to regain feeling in his arm, he asked Frank if he was ready to set sail. "Ha ha, yes, I'm ready, but I still have crew flying in. It looks like your ship will be the first one to leave port again," Frank said with a big grin. "I guess so, but I thought you wouldn't leave for a couple more weeks?" Thomas inquired. "Well, you've kicked everyone into gear. No one wants to get left behind for the third year in a row. The other captains and I are all geared up now to go for the full fishing season. I hope we see each other out there. I've been looking forward to catching halibut," Frank shared. Smiling, Thomas patted Frank on the arm and said, "I'm just happy you noticed that there's more than salmon out there." Frank bellowed with laughter and gave Thomas a hearty pat on the back that almost made him fall over. Frank wished Thomas a good season and went on his way.

Thomas observed Frank as he made his way towards his own ship, the "Salmon Spirit," a grand vessel that perfectly reflected the captain's persona. As Thomas was about to begin walking, he heard a voice behind him. "Oh, look who it is, Captain Thomas, the man who can do anything and sail everywhere," the voice said. Thomas turned to see Susan Flores, a brown-haired Hispanic woman who captained the "Polar Seeker."

Thomas approached Susan with a warm smile and inquired about her well-being. "Don't try to be kind to me after what you've done," Susan retorted. Thomas, taken aback, asked her to explain. "Oh, don't act innocent. You know how much money we all had to spend this year because of you!" Susan exclaimed. Thomas let out a deep sigh and began to walk away. "Sure, walk away, Thomas. But be cautious. The other captains won't be as forgiving as I am," Susan yelled over the bustling crowd. As Thomas moved through the crowd, he felt the weight of accusatory stares from the other sailors. While he usually blended in effortlessly, being singled out made him feel like the most wanted man in the marina.

11

After successfully maneuvering through the bustling harbor, Thomas reached the formidable Harbor Master's office. He knocked on the door and was invited in by a voice from inside. Upon entering, he was greeted by Dennis Collins, an older man with thin, disheveled blond hair, and Aaron Garcia, a man with smooth, black hair of Hispanic descent. As Thomas closed the door behind him, Dennis asked, "How can I assist you, Thomas?"

"I was hoping to confirm that all my paperwork is in order so I can set sail on Monday," Thomas replied. Aaron slid open a drawer, extracted a sheaf of papers, and handed them to Dennis, stating, "I already approved everything two days ago, so he should be good to go." After scrutinizing the paperwork, Dennis signed off on it, but not without a cautionary remark: "You know the other captains aren't too pleased with you." As he made copies of the documents, Dennis continued, "Yes, I've heard," Thomas replied. After receiving the copies, Thomas thanked them and made his exit. As he left, he couldn't help but notice the smirks on Dennis and Aaron's faces. Despite their amusement, Thomas was certain of one thing: when a captain becomes the enemy of others, trouble is bound to follow.

12

After departing from the Harbor Master's office, Thomas made a beeline for Seafarer's Repairs, the premier boat repair facility at the Marina. Having placed an order for additional upgrades to his ship the previous year following a highly profitable season, Thomas was intent on further enhancing the ship to improve the crew's quality of life.

Thomas made his way to the open-air shipyard, where he observed a row of ships being tended to by repairmen welding metal, sawing wood, and pressure washing the boat hulls. With a clear destination in mind, Thomas located the office shed where he anticipated finding the person he was looking for. As he approached the door, it suddenly swung open, revealing Johnathan Jackson standing before him. Johnathan, a formidable figure with a dark complexion, hailed from Kodiak Point as well. He was the captain of the Arctic Voyager, the only other ship led by a black captain. Standing behind Johnathan was Nathan Kelly, a robust white man and the captain of the Kodiak King. Despite extending a greeting, Thomas was met with a dismissive shove from Johnathan, accompanied by a menacing glare. Nathan, following Johnathan's lead, tersely remarked, "We'll be seeing you out there." It was evident to Thomas that there was no goodwill behind that statement.

Thomas entered the room and immediately spotted the man he had been searching for: Timothy Diaz, a jovial, Hispanic man with a substantial belly. "Look at you, Thomas, always making friends," Timothy remarked with a chuckle. Walking closer to the counter, Thomas replied, "It's not my fault for wanting to push the boundaries and achieve more during the season than everyone else." Timothy laughed and retorted, "You might be right, but when you outperform everyone and make them look like fools, you'll get all the blame."

As Timothy's words echoed in his mind, Thomas reminisced about an incident from two years ago when he had proposed sailing for the entire season to pursue Halibut, Herring, Salmon, Cod, Rockfish, and Crab. He recalled how the crew had initially resisted the idea, leading to some members leaving. However, those who stayed had reaped greater benefits than anyone else. The crew had grown, and their profits had soared. In the first year, no one had paid them any attention, but by the second year, Thomas had unintentionally put himself and his crew in the spotlight. Other captains had begun spending money to upgrade their ships, although it wasn't necessary. Yet, in the end, someone had to take the blame.

Thomas inquired, "Were you able to complete the upgrades on my ship?" Timothy produced some documents and assured Thomas that all the requested modifications had been made. He then asked Thomas to sign some paperwork to finalize the process. Concerned, Timothy asked Thomas if he was sure everything was okay, as he had attracted significant attention. Thomas, with a smirk, replied, "I thought you'd be pleased; I've brought you more business." Timothy chuckled and thanked him. As Thomas finished signing, Vincent Gomez, a diminutive Hispanic man in charge of refueling ships, entered the room. Vincent appeared uneasy as he confirmed that he had fueled up Thomas's ship the previous day. Both Timothy and Thomas exchanged a concerned glance. In response to Timothy's question, Vincent nervously revealed that other captains had asked him to delay refueling Thomas's ship. Although he had refused, he was anxious about potential repercussions. Infuriated, Timothy slammed his fist on the counter and declared that he would not tolerate any foul play by his employees or others. Despite Thomas's attempts to placate him, Timothy remained visibly agitated. Despite this, they bid each other farewell, and Thomas left the office.

As Thomas walked along the dock, he found solace in the tranquility of the surroundings. The hustle and bustle of the crowd allowed him to blend in unnoticed, giving him a sense of relief that he wouldn't have to engage with anyone else for the rest of the day or the entire week. Although he was indifferent to the potential disapproval of other captains, the thought of anyone trying to manipulate his crew for their own gain irked him. Fortunately, he had cultivated valuable connections, allowing him to focus on what lay ahead. His thoughts turned to his beloved ship, a vessel that had been a part of his life since childhood. The ship, named the Northern Star, was not just his pride and joy but also a symbol of safety and security for him and his crew. Standing in front of the ship, he felt a deep sense of belonging and gratitude for the haven it provided him, both on the open sea and in his heart.

13

As Thomas drew closer to his vessel, the Northern Star, a 75-foot Jensen Maritime Seiner, a wave of nostalgia washed over him. The two-tone ship boasted a sleek white upper half and a striking, contrasting bright red bottom. Placing his hand on the ship's surface, Thomas savored the flood of memories from his countless experiences aboard. However, it was time to shift gears from reminiscing to assuming the role of captain and inspecting the new upgrades he had commissioned.

As he stepped onto the ship, he surveyed the main deck, making sure that all the fishing equipment was still in good condition. Thomas was particularly interested in inspecting the new purse winch he had ordered to improve the fishing efficiency. The previous winch had struggled to handle the volume of fish Thomas aimed to catch, so the need for a larger, more robust winch was evident. He carefully tested the hydraulic system and observed that the new winch effortlessly raised and lowered the freshly ordered nets. After conducting several tests, Thomas was content with the performance and proceeded to conduct a thorough check of the entire vessel.

He descended below deck and headed towards the Fish Hold, a spacious room where the crew stored the freshly caught fish. The area was well-maintained, with ample room for the two fish processors. Everything met Thomas's high standards, and he couldn't spot any issues. Consulting his notepad, Thomas marked off the Fish Hold from his inspection list, feeling a sense of satisfaction at the efficient system in place. With that task completed, he proceeded to the Galley.

The galley, as we sailors call it, was impeccably clean and fully compliant with regulations. Thomas brought in a professional cleaning crew to thoroughly clean the entire ship, paying special attention to the kitchen. He couldn't deny that Chris tended to make a bit of a mess whenever he cooked. Walking through the room, Thomas meticulously checked and tested every aspect of the kitchen - from turning on the stove and running water from the sink to inspecting the refrigerator to ensure everything was in perfect order. Satisfied, Thomas smiled and marked the galley off his checklist.

Thomas strolled into the adjacent room, which served as the crew's dining area. The Mess Area was spacious, comfortably accommodating 15 sailors with ample seating for all. Thomas meticulously inspected the tables and chairs, ensuring they were sturdy and in good condition. After thoroughly assessing the area, he was satisfied that everything was in order and could confidently check the Mess Area off his list.

As Thomas made his way down to the Crew Quarters, he could feel a sense of anticipation building up. This room was where the entire crew, except for the first mate and the captain, spent their resting hours. The once cramped space had undergone a remarkable transformation, filled with bunk beds and small closets. Thanks to the substantial profits the ship had generated over the past two years, Thomas had taken it upon himself to carry out extensive upgrades. The room had been completely remodeled, with the bunk beds replaced by individual beds, each equipped with storage bins underneath. Additionally, a locker was placed on each bed, providing the crew with ample space to store their belongings. Thomas hoped that the crew would appreciate these changes, as they would no longer have to worry about sleeping in close quarters.

As Thomas strolled through the hallway, he made his way from the Crew Quarters to the Engie Room. Upon opening the door, he was greeted by the impressive sight of the ship's engine, generators, and pumps. Taking a moment to carefully inspect each component, Thomas ensured that everything was in proper working order. Being well aware of the unpredictability of the sea, he meticulously checked the storage room to confirm the availability of replacement parts and essential repair tools. Satisfied that everything was in place, Thomas felt confident in their readiness for the journey ahead. With the Engine Room successfully checked off his list, he knew that he had one final stop to make before departing.

Thomas made his way to the Wheel House, the nerve center of the vessel. This was the space where navigation, communication, and the operation of the ship were overseen. It was a room filled with memories for Thomas, having spent countless hours in there with his father, who had been training him to take over one day. As Thomas opened the door, a wave of nostalgia washed over him. He ran his hand over the radar, reminiscing about the days when he was a young boy, full of curiosity and questions about the equipment. Moving on, he checked the radio for functionality and picked up the satellite phone to ensure it had a dial tone. The faint sound of a ring echoed through the room as he placed the phone back down. Next, he inspected the steering controls, the very same controls where he had taken his first steps as captain-in-training. Looking out at the expanse of the sea, he observed the sun casting its warm glow over the horizon. Lost in thought, Thomas decided to step out onto the main deck, craving the feel of the fresh sea air against his face.

Thomas stood at the edge of the ship, gazing out over the starboard bow with his eyes fixed on the distant horizon. As he closed his eyes, he anticipated the gentle touch of the breeze. Suddenly, the wind intensified. Philip had warned Thomas about an uneasiness in the air. Thomas couldn't shake the feeling that something ominous loomed on the horizon, leaving him uncertain about how to prepare himself for what lay ahead.

14

Thomas devoted an entire week to meticulously plotting the route for his crew. He meticulously studied weather channels, analyzed the data provided by Ralph, and kept Philip's advice in mind. Thomas couldn't shake the feeling that something was amiss despite his efforts. Reports from the new station indicated storms brewing in the middle of the Pacific Ocean, a location where Ralph's data from last year suggested such events were unlikely. While he initially attributed it to Mother Nature's whims, Thomas couldn't dismiss his concerns. He planned to navigate around the storm, but unease still gnawed at him. The halibut season wouldn't endure the storm's duration, leaving Thomas with lingering uncertainties.

In the middle of the week, Thomas found himself restless in bed, his mind consumed by a haunting dream. In the dream, he witnessed a calamity befalling his crew as their ship sank, and he was unable to save anyone. The dream felt incredibly vivid as he helplessly watched his crew members vanish one by one until only James remained. As the water rose around them, Thomas clung desperately to James' sleeve, urging him not to let go. However, James's visage began to fade despite Thomas's frantic pleas until he eventually disappeared altogether.

Thomas awoke to the sight of Mary standing over him, urgently calling out to wake him up. He rubbed his eyes and sat up, realizing that he had fallen asleep on the couch surrounded by scattered chart paper. "Are you okay? You were shouting in your sleep," Mary said with concern. Now fully awake, Thomas rested his head in his hands and took a deep breath. "It was just a recurring nightmare. I often have them before we set sail," he explained. Mary sat down beside him and observed, "But this seemed more intense than usual, Thomas. You're drenched in sweat, and you look unwell." Thomas glanced down at his sweaty clothes, puzzled by his physical state. "Is this about the other captain? Are you worried about something happening to us out there?" Mary inquired. Placing a reassuring hand on her shoulder, Thomas replied, "They may not be fond of me, but there's still an unspoken code." As he prepared to stand up, Mary gently urged him to stay seated. "Okay, but does Johnathan abide by that code?" she pressed. Thomas leaned back, reflecting on the complex history between him and Johnathan. "Johnathan's father and mine never saw eye to eye. They were always competing over who had the best fishing season. I tried to befriend Johnathan when we were young, but his father's animosity toward mine persisted. Johnathan assumed command of his father's ship two years before I took over my dad's vessel. During that period, his ship was the top earner in Kodiak Point until I arrived. I've dreamt of captaining a ship since I was five, and I had ambitious plans from the start. One of those decisions was to sail for the entire fishing season, catching everything the sea had to offer. It was a risky gamble, and my father disapproved, but James supported my endeavor. Within a year, I earned ten times more than all the other ships. Initially, no one paid much attention, but when it happened a second time, all eyes were on me. Johnathan already harbored resentment, but surpassing him as the top earner pushed him over the edge. Nevertheless, I can't control others' emotions, so I never bothered with them. Despite his dislike for me, Johnathan still adhered to a code."

Thomas gazed into his wife's eyes, reassuring her that everything would be alright. Despite his words, Mary remained anxious and pleaded with him to stay safe. "I promise I will," Thomas assured her. Unconvinced, Mary forced a smile and replied, "I'll remember that."

15

The entire crew was gathered in the dimly lit back room of Kodiak Bar & Grill, eagerly awaiting Thomas's arrival. "Where's Thomas? I've got a date before we set sail tomorrow," Joshua inquired. "Well, if the girl's got any sense, she won't stick around for long," Andrew quipped. Laughter filled the air as drinks flowed and camaraderie abounded. Meanwhile, James observed from the corner, quietly taking in the shared laughter and nostalgic tales of sailing with Thomas's father. "Thomas's old man was something else. He'd sail into any storm without hesitation. A brave captain who never shied away from risks," Chris recounted, holding the attention of the others. Before Chris could finish, Thomas walked into the room, instantly silencing the boisterous gathering.

Thomas gazed around the room, his eyes resting on Chris, who had somehow shrunk to the size of a mouse. A small smile played on Thomas's lips as he addressed the crew. "My father was a brave risk-taker, but I'm cut from a different cloth. Chris, save your stories for when we're out at sea," he said. Chris nodded, acknowledging Thomas as the captain, and fell in line with the rest of the crew.

Standing at the front of the room, Thomas commanded everyone's attention as he laid out the plan. "We'll be at sea for three-week stretches, then back to port for a week with your families," he informed them. "Our target for the season is halibut. Here are your assignments." He proceeded to assign roles: James as the deck boss, Michael, Richard, Joseph, Charles, Paul, and Steven as the deckhand crew, Matthew and Andrew as fish processors, Daniel as the bait master, and Chris as the cook. Mark would serve as the navigator, Joshua would be the radio operator, and William would be the engineer. Lastly, Thomas welcomed the two new recruits, David Davis and Anthony Miller, urging the crew to show them the ropes.

As the group gathered, everyone enthusiastically shouted "welcome," making both Anthoney and David feel truly embraced. "Tomorrow is the big day, and the boat is ready for you to start loading your gear," announced Thomas. James chimed in, warning that anyone not on the boat by 5:00 am would be left behind. The crew acknowledged the instructions, and Thomas urged them to have fun and enjoy themselves before bidding them farewell. With a resounding "Yes, captain!" the crew dispersed to chat and unwind. Thomas approached James and confided, "We need to keep a close watch on our crew; I have a bad feeling about something." Taken aback, James inquired, "Do you think someone will endanger the crew?" Thomas scanned the area and replied, "I'm not concerned about the crew; I'm worried about the weather." With a reassuring hand on James's shoulder, Thomas left.

16

At 4:15 am, the crew was bustling about, loading up the Northern Star and bidding farewell to their families. Thomas sat in the bridge, gazing out over the vast expanse of the ocean as he waited for his crew to finish their goodbyes. Lost in thought, he couldn't shake his concern about the looming storms and the peculiar winds that Philip had warned him about. The nightmares that had plagued him all week were also weighing heavily on his mind. While he was accustomed to them during this time of the year, Mary's intuition had made him acutely aware that something was amiss.

As James strolled into the room, he informed Thomas that the ship was prepared for departure. Thomas, who had been lost in his thoughts, refocused and responded affirmatively. Concerned by Thomas's distant demeanor, James gave him a lingering look before exiting the room. Thomas then took to the intercom and announced the commencement of their departure, urging the sailors to man their stations. As the crew hurried to their designated spots, Thomas skillfully maneuvered the Northern Star out of port. Glancing back towards the dock, he caught sight of his wife Mary, still in her pajamas and pink bunny slippers. Despite bidding her farewell earlier that morning, Thomas felt a rush of joy upon seeing her. His mind cleared as he glimpsed what he cherished most about home. Thomas blew her a kiss, which she playfully caught and tucked into her pocket. Smiling, he redirected his focus to the vast expanse of the ocean. Upon James's return, Thomas declared, "Let's get started."

ACT 2

INTO THE ABYSS

1

As the crew settled into their quarters and began unpacking, the atmosphere was filled with excitement and laughter. Some of the men were claiming beds and exchanging jokes about the upcoming adventure. "Just wait; I'm determined to catch the largest salmon this year," declared Steven confidently. Daniel, with a mischievous smirk, retorted, "Not unless

I use you as bait to lure them in your direction." This sparked laughter from some of the crew members while others busied themselves with unpacking and hanging up pictures in their new lockers.

Curious about their new surroundings, David asked, "So, you guys have never had these kinds of beds before?" Michael responded, "No, Thomas must have just bought these before we all had to sleep on bunk beds."

Then, Anthony hesitantly brought up a more sensitive topic, "I hope this isn't out of place, but I've been wondering why Thomas is the captain instead of James. From what I understand, both James and Thomas's father co-owned this boat when they started." The room fell silent, and Anthony feared he had overstepped. Only when he noticed the crew's diverted gazes did he realize they were not looking at him. Anthony turned around to find James standing behind him, casting a formidable shadow. Despite Anthony's quick apology, James simply raised his hand to silence him.

"That's a valid question, Antoney, but don't worry. A long time ago, I realized that I didn't want to be a captain; the responsibility is too great for most men. However, Thomas is exceptional - he stands above all the rest. All I want is to gaze at the sea and return to my little girls. Oh, and my wife, of course." Laughter filled the room as James continued. "Our captain wants everyone to gather in the mess hall. He wants to brief everyone about tomorrow." The crew promptly stood up and replied, "Yes, sir." James smiled and exited the room. After he left, Chris approached Antoney and said, "You might be new to the crew, but never question who should be the captain of this boat." Antoney nodded, indicating that he understood.

After everyone had finished unpacking, they gathered in the mess hall, eagerly awaiting the arrival of their captain. Thomas entered the room with a warm smile and greeted each crew member. As he took his seat, he positioned himself to have a clear view of everyone. "Hello, everyone. I apologize for the rush, but I want to inform you that we will be setting off at full steam ahead tomorrow. Our target is Hailbut, and I aim to start early. I need everyone to prepare their stations for tomorrow. Daniel, I need you to start by throwing out bait. I want the fish to become accustomed to the scent of our boat before we begin fishing. Any questions?" Thomas inquired, but the room remained silent. "Very well. David and Anthony, I want you to accompany James and learn the ropes of deck work. You'll serve as deckhands until I determine where to best utilize your skills. Now, everyone, get to work, and Chris, dinner will be ready in a few hours, correct?" Thomas asked. Chris grinned and replied, "Yes, Captain." With a smile, Thomas dismissed the crew, signaling the end of the meeting.

2

As James led the way, David and Anthony listened intently as he explained the various tasks and operations that take place in each room. They observed the processing and storage of the fish and then proceeded to the engine room, where James elaborated on how the ship is powered. James also mentioned that they would be working in multiple areas until Thomas determines where they will be most effective. David appeared eager, while Anthony remained silent, still hesitant to ask his earlier question.

They finally reached the deck, where James presented them with the purse seine net, a large circular net specifically designed for catching schools of fish. James went on to explain the use of hydraulic winches for raising and lowering the nets and then demonstrated how they would unload the fish once the net was brought on board. Both Anthoney and David paid careful attention, and James even allowed them to practice until it was time to join Thomas on the bridge. As they looked at each other, they set down the nets and followed James up to the bridge, where they found Thomas seated at a desk, taking a sip of water.

"Hey, how are you both doing?" Thomas inquired. David and Anthony assured him that they were feeling fine. With a smile, Thomas added, "That's great. I have one more question for you. What motivated you to join my crew?" Both of them hesitated, and James encouraged them to share their thoughts. David spoke up first, stating, "I aspire to captain my own ship one day, and I believe I need to learn from the best. I want to learn from someone who challenges the status quo, and everywhere I go, I hear that you, Thomas, are the best. I feel that I need to be here to study under your guidance, sir." Thomas nodded and turned to look at Anthony.

Anthony paused, inhaling deeply before speaking. "I'm seeking a fresh start. Life down south was exhilarating, but it was also easy to fall into trouble. I want to establish stability here. I need something to bring order to my life, a situation that demands my unwavering focus without any distractions. I believed I could find that up north, perhaps with this group," he mused. Thomas acknowledged his words with a nod before making his way to the bridge window.

Thomas began to say, "I always ask the same question to everyone I bring on my ship. Most people say they want to make money, but those who do are not the right fit for my crew. When I first took over, we lost half of our crew because they thought I was asking for too much. I will always be grateful for the ones who stayed. They weren't concerned about money or hard work; they simply wanted to be out at sea, leaving their daily problems behind. Just like you both, I am not focusing on money but on my own life goals. If you choose to stay, you'll be part of my family, and as part of my family, I promise that no matter what, I will ensure you make it back home."

Anthony then questioned, "Sir, are you sure you can make that promise?" Thomas responded with a smile, "That promise is why I can do my job so well. Now, James, it's dinner time. Take these two down to the mess hall and get some food. Tomorrow is going to be a big day."

3

The early morning air is filled with the sound of mechanical arms whistling as they drop nets into the water. Thomas skillfully positions the boat and studies the radar to ensure it is directly over the school of fish. The nets are dropped, and soon James raises them up, filling them to the brim with Halibut. Meanwhile, the deckhands are busy unloading the fish and preparing the nets for another drop. Danial is hard at work, dropping buckets of bait into the ocean to attract more fish. The greenhorns are impressing James, who radios to Thomas to keep the boat steady.

Below the deck, Matthew and Andrew are working quickly to process the fish, keeping pace with the crew on deck. After a few hours, Thomas announces over the intercom that it's enough for today. Everyone stops and begins to break down the gear and wash down the deck. Chris emerges with sandwiches, signaling it's time for lunch. The deckhands eagerly grab a sandwich while James takes out his notepad to assess how the first day went. Thomas descends from the bridge to check on everyone. He walks over to James and inquires about the crew's performance. "They did better than I expected. We've met today's quota, and it's not even 11 am yet," James reports. Thomas pats him on the shoulder and then approaches Anthoney and David. "How was it for you two?" Thomas asks. They both indicate it wasn't too bad and express their desire to improve when they resume. "I apologize for any confusion. I have a system where we only need to catch a certain amount of fish per day. Once we reach that number, we spend the remainder of the time getting ready for tomorrow and unwinding. The sea can be rough, and I want my crew to be at their best," Thomas explains.

David was surprised and remarked, "I've never heard of someone do-ing that." Thomas replied, "It's about maintaining balance; there are plenty of fish out there, so there's no need to rush." David nodded in understanding and continued to enjoy his sandwich.

James finished jotting down his notes and glanced up, only to be taken aback by the sight of something bright yel-low floating in the water. Intrigued, he moved closer for a better look and real-ized it was a yellow life raft with an arm dangling over the side. "Thomas, there's a life raft off the port bow!" James called out. Thomas hurried over, spotted the raft, and swiftly ran to the bridge and steered the boat closer to it. Meanwhile, Richard dashed to grab the medical bag as the rest of the crew joined in to hoist the life raft onto the deck.

Once the raft was secured, Thomas rushed down from the bridge. James carefully examined the two men in white lab coats and pressed his ear against their chests. "I hear a heartbeat. We need to get them inside," he urged. Richard arrived with the medical bag, with Thomas following closely behind. Thomas instructed Paul and

Steven to escort the men down to the crew's quarters and make them comfortable. "Yes, Captain," they acknowledged, swiftly carrying out the orders. Meanwhile, Thomas radioed Joshua to contact the Coast Guard and inform them that they had found two men who were lost at sea.

Thomas observed as the scientists in their lab coats descended below deck. Just as he was about to speak to James, a powerful gust of wind struck Thomas, nearly knocking him off balance. He turned and saw a massive fog bank rolling in, accompanied by a raging storm with lightning that illuminated the sky.

4

The storm was rapidly approaching, and Thomas couldn't fathom its origin. He had deliberately charted a course to avoid the storm based on the news reports. Turning to James, he inquired about the unusual nature of the storm. "This isn't normal - I've never seen a storm accompanied by such thick fog. We need to change our course immediately; I won't risk sailing into that," James exclaimed, and Thomas concurred. Urgently, Thomas instructed the crew to secure the deck. Rushing back to the bridge, he was startled to find the storm upon them already. "How did it close in on us so quickly? I was just observing it," Thomas muttered to himself. He contacted James over the radio and sought an update. "The rain is pouring down heavily, and the fog obscures our visibility - I can barely see 20 feet ahead," James reported. Reassuring James, Thomas vowed to navigate them out of the storm.

James and the other deckhands struggled to maintain their balance as the relentless waves rocked the boat. James urgently radioed Thomas to try to stabilize the boat, but the overpowering force of the waves made it nearly impossible. Through the intercom, Thomas instructed everyone to seek shelter below deck. Just as James and the others were making their way down, a bone-chilling roar echoed through the air, freezing them in their tracks. "What was that?" Anthony asked, but before anyone could respond, something powerful collided with the boat from beneath, causing everyone to tumble. As Thomas peered out, he caught sight of a massive, dark figure lurking under the water. "What in the world is that?" he pondered aloud.

James struggled to his feet and urgently instructed everyone to seek shelter below deck, but his words seemed to fall on deaf ears. Frustration turned to fear as he gazed up and saw the source of everyone's terror. Meanwhile, Thomas attempted to radio the men to take cover, only to find them all staring upwards in shock. Following their gaze, he, too, was transfixed by the sight of two eerie red lights piercing through the fog.

5

The crew stood in stunned silence, their eyes fixed on the ominous red lights above. Confusion ran through their minds as David spoke up, "What is that?" Suddenly, the lights vanished, and a massive disturbance beneath the water caught their attention. James, jolting back to reality, swiftly ordered the crew to take cover below deck. As they scrambled to obey, a tremendous force collided with the side of the boat, sending the crew sprawling once more. Despite Thomas's efforts to steer, the situation proved overwhelming. He urgently radioed James, emphasizing the need to stop the relentless assault on the vessel. Surveying the chaotic scene, James spotted a box of flares sliding across the deck. Racing over, he retrieved four flares and swiftly launched two—one into the air and another off the side of the boat, where a shadow had caught his eye. A menacing hiss and roar pierced the air as something colossal began to surface from the depths. With both the crew on deck and Thomas on the bridge transfixed a colossal serpent slowly emerged, casting a chilling spectacle upon them all.

The monstrous creature loomed over the boat, its head resembling that of a dragon with scaly horns protruding from either side. Its long, weathered green neck bore a resemblance to the ancient dinosaurs depicted in old movies. As the creature opened its mouth, a long, red tongue slid over its numerous sharp teeth, giving the impression that it could easily snap the boat in half. Standing at a towering height of 40 feet, the creature peered down at the boat with intense, burning red eyes that seemed to penetrate Thomas's very soul. His heart raced as he felt the creature's gaze fixate on him as if it were peering into the depths of hell itself. Thomas was overcome with panic, his mind racing as he searched for a way to ensure the safety of his crew in the face of this terrifying adversary.

Thomas took to the radio and told James to fire a flare right into that creature's eye. James heard the order, grabbed the flare, and aimed right for the large, bright red eye that was looking down on them. James fired, and the flare landed right on target. The creature roared into the sky, shattering the bridge window, and the wind rushed in with the rain following behind it. As the creature moved back, Thomas put the ship in full throttle and roared past the large serpent. Thomas radioed down to William and told him to keep an eye on the engine. Thomas knew he was pushing it, but he had to.

As he glanced behind him, Thomas locked eyes with the menacing monster once again. With little time to spare, he quickly radioed James, "Prepare the nets and drop them off the port bow. Be ready to release the anchor on my command." James sprang into action, barking orders to his crew to ready the nets. "Why are we doing this?" Anthony questioned. "Just follow the captain's orders," Michael snapped back. Meanwhile, James operated the arms and released the net into the water while Michael stood poised by the anchor release, awaiting Thomas's command. "Everything is set," James radioed Thomas, who replied, "Wait for my signal." Keeping a watchful eye on the creature gaining speed, Thomas watched as its head disappeared underwater – just as he had hoped. "Drop anchor!" Thomas bellowed over the radio, and Michael swiftly pulled the switch. The crew listened intently as the chains clattered down the port side of the boat, all eyes fixed on their captain's next move. With a determined gaze, Thomas turned back to the task at hand, urging the ship to maintain full throttle as he caught a glimpse of the creature's glowing red eyes beneath the water's surface.

Thomas drew in a deep breath and whispered, "Please, let this work." At that moment, the anchor snagged the bottom, and the boat veered sharply to the left. Thomas swiftly spun the wheel, causing the boat to execute a 180-degree turn in the water. "Cut the anchor!" he bellowed into the radio, and Michael swiftly obeyed. As the anchor was released, the boat now faced the monstrous creature. Instructing James to stabilize the net over the radio, Thomas watched in horror as the creature rammed into the net, surfacing right beside them and tearing the winch arm right off the boat. James took his last flare and fired it again, right into the monster's eye. The monster roared again, but this time, Thomas had the boat speeding past, reaching the other end of the storm. He looked back to see that the creature was still tangled in the net, trying to get free.

The edge of the fog came into view, and Thomas didn't ease up as the ship pierced through the mist. The crew, still in shock, watched as the fog they had just left continued to show eerie images of a mysterious creature every time lightning struck. Thomas radioed down to William in the engine room, saying, "Whatever you do, keep the engine running." William responded, "Yes, captain." As the fog started to fade in the distance, Thomas and the rest of the crew on deck could still see the red eyes watching them from the dissipating mist.

6

Thomas remained at the helm, his hands firmly gripping the wheel as he tried to process the shocking events that had just unfolded. Suddenly, James burst onto the bridge, exclaiming, "What in God's name was that?" Thomas, his eyes wide with disbelief, could only respond, "I was about to ask you the same thing." As James examined the damage to the windows, he marveled at how a powerful force had shattered them.

Concerned for the crew's well-being, Thomas inquired, "Is everyone okay? Did anyone get hurt?" James reassured him, "Everyone is unharmed but shaken. The rest of the crew is unsettled and curious about what transpired on deck. I've asked Michael to retrieve the security footage and gather the crew in the mess hall while I come up here to speak with you."

Thomas nodded thoughtfully and engaged the boat's auto-pilot, instructing, "Inform everyone to convene in the mess hall. We need to discuss what just occurred." James, still apprehensive, inquired, "Do you think we're out of danger now?" Thomas scanned the surroundings and replied, "The storm has subsided, and the creature seems to have vanished with it. However, we must continue to port without stopping. Tell Joshua to notify the Coast Guard that we will be returning with the scientists on board."

James hesitated before asking, "What about the sea monster? Shouldn't we report that too?" Thomas shook his head, "They won't believe us without evidence. We need to convene a meeting with all the captains and present the video footage. No ships will set sail until we address this situation." James agreed,

"I'll gather everyone in the mess hall. I'll see you there." With that, Thomas took a moment to compose himself before making his way to the mess hall, the fear of a sea monster attack lingering in his mind.

7

Thomas strode into the mess hall, his crew gathered around the TV, their eyes fixed on the screen displaying the chaos unfolding above deck. As the video came to an end, a heavy silence fell over the room. Spotting Thomas, Paul spoke up, "Captain, what was that thing?" Taking a seat, Thomas declared, "I don't know what it was, but our voyage is in jeopardy.

We won't rest until we're all safely back home. I need everyone to focus on repairing any damages so we can make it back without a hitch." The crew nodded in agreement, but Daniel raised a concern, "What about the sea monster? And the halibut in the ice hold? What do we do about that?" Thomas fixed him with a stern look that silenced Daniel. "Our priority is getting everyone home," he stated firmly before heading back to the bridge. Before anyone else could speak, James stepped forward, urging the crew, "Don't question the captain's orders, especially after he just saved all of us. Now, let's get to work."

8

The Northern Star has returned to port after a night of continuous sailing. As the boat approaches the dock, the other sailors and harbor workers are inspecting the damages. Enormous gashes and dents run along the side of the ship, and someone has noticed that one of the winches has been torn away from the ship. Dennis Collins and the rest of the Coast Guard are waiting for the ship to finish docking so that they can assess what happened.

The ship was safely docked, but the atmosphere was tense as the Coast Guards hurriedly unloaded medical supplies, their movements accompanied by the distant wail of approaching ambulances. James swiftly directed the Coast Guards to the Crews Quarters, while Thomas made his way over to meet with Dennis. "What happened to your ship?" Dennis inquired, but Thomas seemed preoccupied. "I need to convene a meeting with all the captains and the Chairmen of the Fishermen coop. Also, get the mayor -

he needs to see the footage," Thomas insisted, striding purposefully. Dennis stopped him, puzzled, "Hey, what happened, Thomas? Why does your boat look like it was attacked by a monster?" Thomas spun back around, his eyes filled with anger, reiterating, "Gather all the captains, the chairmen, and the mayor." Shocked, Dennis agreed, "Okay, we'll meet at the Harbor Authority Office." Thomas expressed his gratitude and inquired, "Does that room have a TV?" "Yes, we have a projector. Are you okay?" Dennis asked, concerned. Thomas took a deep breath and replied, "No, I'm not. I need to see my wife."

9

Thomas was eager to call his wife, but first, he had to share the footage of the incident involving his crew with the other captains. He patiently waited in the Harbor Authority office, where a projector was set up to show the footage from the flash drive. James entered the room and informed Thomas that the scientists were now at the hospital while the rest of the crew had left for home. Thomas acknowledged the news and tried to comprehend the nature of the monstrous entity that seemed to control the storm. Before he could dwell on these questions, the other captains arrived, ready for the discussion.

All the captains of Kodiak Point were present, including Frank Lee, Susan, Nathen, and a few others. Even Johnathan made an appearance. Following them was an older white man with a long snow-white beard, Matthew Nelson, the chairman of the Fisherman Coop. Alongside him was our mayor, Arthur Daiz, a smug, business-like Hispanic man who strolled in with greasy, slicked-back hair and a cheap three-piece suit. They all took their seats as Dennis stepped to the front of the room. "I'm sure you all saw what happened to Thomas's ship. He has some footage that he'd like to share with us," Dennis announced, giving the floor to Thomas. Standing before a room where most held hatred towards him, Thomas remained unfazed. "I could describe what happened, but it's better if I show you," he said, gesturing for James to hit play on the projector.

As everyone looked on in shock, Thomas stood to the side, watching a sea monster resembling the Loch Ness monster attacking the ship and threatening the crew's survival. The video concluded with the ship sailing away while the monster was ensnared in a net. After a moment of silence, Frank voiced his disbelief, asking if what they had witnessed was real. James, pointing to the ship, replied, "If you don't believe it, look at our vessel." Thomas, concerned for everyone's safety, urged caution, stating, "It's not safe out there. We have no idea what that thing is. We shouldn't sail until we figure out what to do." The room erupted into chaos as captains began shouting at Thomas. One of them accused him of prioritizing profit over lives, referencing his earlier successful haul. "Do you value money more than your lives?" James yelled. Turning to the mayor and the chairman, Thomas awaited their responses.

Matthew expressed his unease, stating that he was not comfortable with anyone sailing at that moment. He suggested locking down the dock. The other captain vehemently protested, claiming that it was unfair, while others insisted that they were willing to take their chances. The mayor, acknowledging that he was not a sailor, observed that the others did not seem concerned about the issue. He decided not to intervene if they wanted to sail.

James confronted the mayor, accusing him of being more concerned about profiting from the sailors than ensuring safety. The mayor, visibly angered, challenged James to stop the captains without the city's support. Tensions rose until Thomas intervened, pleading with the mayor not to let the sailors set sail. The mayor, showing no remorse, walked away, declaring that the dock would remain open. As the other captains cheered and left, they cast dirty looks at James and Thomas.

As the room emptied, only Thomas, James, Frank, Dennis, and Matthew remained. "They are all fools!" James exclaimed. Thomas, with a sigh, turned to Frank and inquired about his plans. "I'm not risking my crew's life. I'm not sailing out tomorrow," Frank declared. Thomas expressed his gratitude, then turned to Dennis, asking if there was anything he could do. Dennis shook his head and replied, "Only the mayor can intervene now. I would lock down the dock, but it's beyond my control." Matthew took a seat and murmured, "May God have mercy on them." Thomas, feeling lost, looked at James and asked for guidance. "There's nothing we can do, Thomas. I'm going home to my wife, and I suggest you do the same," James advised. Thomas took a deep breath and heeded James's

words, realizing that all he wanted was
to embrace his wife and tell her he loved
her.

ACT 3

The Warnng Cry

1

After a tiring day filled with heart-felt conversations with his wife, Thomas fell asleep, only to find himself transported back to the sea in his dreams. He was on a small boat, confronting a monstrous creature amidst the pouring rain. The creature's piercing red eyes seemed to sear into his very soul, holding him captive with fear. It gazed at him with a menacing intensity, almost relishing in Thomas's terror, while he realized there was no escape. In a barely audible whisper, he heard the words, ***"Come to me."***

Thomas jolted awake, his heart pounding in his chest as he let out a piercing scream, "Who are you?" Mary was by his side in an instant, reassuring him that he was safe at home. Thomas drenched in sweat, scanned his room, feeling as though a pair of sinister red eyes were still fixed on him. The digital clock showed 4:15 am. With trembling hands, he reached for his coat, determined to confront the source of his fear. "Where are you going, Thomas?" Mary's concerned voice echoed behind him. As he fastened his coat, he replied, "To see if anyone came to their senses." Without looking back, Thomas bolted down the stairs and out of the house, heading towards the harbor.

2

Thomas descended to the bustling docks, where he observed crews bustling about, preparing to embark on their voyage. Thomas was taken aback by the lack of seriousness with which the crew seemed to be approaching the potentially perilous journey. As he scanned the scene, his eyes settled on James engaged in conversation with a robust, bald, white man. Drawing nearer, Thomas recognized the man as Samuel Reed, the captain of the Coast Guard. Approaching the pair, Thomas inquired of James about the unfolding situation.

"The video has been widely circulated, but unfortunately, only the Frank Lee ship is not setting sail. Everyone else is leaving, with some even departing ahead of schedule to make a statement. They are all foolishly sailing towards their doom," remarked James. Thomas, taken aback, forgot to greet Samuel, but Samuel reassured him not to worry about it. "The Coast Guard is also preparing. I don't agree with anyone leaving, but the Mayor has also shut us down. The most we can do is be ready to rescue anyone who might be in danger," said Samuel. James mentioned that the police are also aware, but the Mayor is holding them back. "So the mayor cares more about his bottom line than the lives of his citizens," Thomas remarked. James nodded and added, "People will ultimately reveal their true colors when it's time to take action."

"Apologies, guys, I must take my leave," Samuel announced. Thomas and James bid him and his crew farewell, and as Samuel departed, Thomas and James remained on the dock, observing the sailors laughing and singing, unaware of the peril ahead.

Suddenly, Thomas spotted Johnathan and hurried over to him. "Johnathan, you can't go. It's too dangerous. Consider your crew," Thomas implored. Ignoring the warning, Johnathan's eyes blazed with fury as he advanced and forcefully pushed Thomas to the ground.

James noticed and rushed over to see what was happening. "You always thought you were better than us, Thomas, and today I'll prove you wrong!" Johnathan shouted. Thomas stood back up and said, "Are you insane? I've never thought that. Think about what you're doing." Johnathan pushed past him and James as he made his way to his ship, the Arctic Voyager. Thomas was about to follow, but James stopped him and said, "Pride comes before the fall."

Thomas and James stood in awe as they watched the ships one by one leaving the dock and setting sail out to sea. The sun was just beginning to rise on the horizon, casting a warm glow over the waters, while the familiar winds that Thomas had felt before brushed heavy against their faces.

3

In the middle of the night, Thomas found himself engulfed in yet another terrifying nightmare. He was stranded at sea, desperately swimming towards the elusive shore as a violent storm raged around him. The howling wind mercilessly whipped the waves, making it impossible for him to make any progress. Just as he began to feel hope slipping away, a looming shadow cast over him. He turned around to come face to face with a monstrous figure, its piercing red eyes boring into his soul. Instead of succumbing to fear, Thomas found himself filled with a growing sense of hatred towards the creature. It was as if he could sense the creature's malevolent enjoyment of his terror. Through the whistling wind, a haunting voice called out to him, ***"Come to me."*** Defiantly, Thomas shouted back, "Why should I?" The monster's mouth opened, and its long, red tongue slithered out as it hissed, ***"I can make it stop."*** Confused, Thomas questioned, "Make what stop?" The monster's eyes glowed even brighter as it declared, ***"This nightmare."***

Thomas was abruptly awakened by the insistent ringing of his phone, pulling him out of a vivid dream. Groggily, he glanced around and saw Mary peacefully asleep beside him. He fumbled to pick up his phone, noticing that it was James calling. "Hello?" he answered. "Thomas, you need to get down to the dock. Ships are returning, and some haven't made it back," James urgently informed him. Thomas assured James that he would be there soon, ending the call before getting out of bed to change. Mary stirred awake, inquiring about the commotion. Thomas relayed James' message and explained that he needed to head down to the dock. "Please be careful, Thomas," Mary urged. Thomas agreed, tenderly kissed her on the cheek, and swiftly made his way out of the house.

4

Thomas arrived at the dock, where the area was illuminated by flashing blue and red lights, with police officers scattered everywhere. His gaze fell upon the ships sailing into the half-destroyed ports, bearing deep gashes that looked as if they had been bitten into by enormous teeth. As he ventured further, he spotted a tall, black woman with curly hair, holding a clipboard and directing the chaotic scene. Drawing closer, he recognized her as Zoey Thomas, the head doctor at the hospital. "Zoey, what's happening here?" Thomas inquired. Turning to face him, she sighed, "Hey, Thomas. I'm sorry that people didn't heed your warnings. The hospital is going to be overflowing tonight." As Thomas observed the sailors being loaded into vans and trucks, preparing to be transported to the hospital, the gravity of the situation began to sink in.

"Today is a somber day indeed," Thomas remarked as he turned around and came face to face with James. "How many ships managed to return?"

Thomas inquired, to which James responded, "Not enough." Just as more ships were coming in, Samuel appeared with Dennis. "I've spoken to the Mayor, and the dock is now officially on lockdown," Dennis announced. James expressed frustration, exclaiming, "He should have done that from the start!" Trying to calm James down, Samuel agreed, "I understand your frustration. We were only able to rescue a few crews as ships began to sink." When Thomas inquired about the fate of Johnathan's ship, Samuel sadly replied, "We didn't make it in time. His ship was already destroyed when we arrived. One of my men will notify his wife."

The impact of the new revelation hit Thomas like a ton of bricks. He couldn't shake the feeling that he could have done more to prevent the situation with him and the other captains. Thomas fought back tears as James comforted him, placing a reassuring hand on his back. "We'll find a way through this, Thomas," James said.

Thomas regained his composure and gazed out at the horizon. His jaw dropped, and he tried to speak, but no words came out. Everyone wondered what was wrong with him. Then, Thomas pointed his finger toward the sea and uttered, "The fog." As he spoke, everyone turned around and noticed a fog beginning to form, accompanied by an impending thunderstorm. James exclaimed, "It can't be." They all watched in awe as the faint silhouette of a creature with a long neck and glowing red ears started to emerge from the fog.

Everyone stood frozen on the dock, their faces etched with fear. Sailors, dockworkers, medical teams, and police alike were petrified as the long-necked monster emerged before their eyes. James's urgent shout shattered the trance, prompting everyone to start moving hastily. Dennis's voice joined in, urging everyone to clear the dock, but Thomas remained rooted to the spot, transfixed by the storm that had halted just 10 miles from the pier. As he gazed out, he found himself locking eyes with the creature, its fiery gaze reminiscent of the eyes that had haunted his dreams.

5

In the grip of another terrify-ing nightmare, Thomas tosses and turns in his bed. Once again, he finds himself lost at sea, battling against the relentless force of the water. Struggling to swim upward, an invisible power seems to drag him down, heightening his struggle. In the murky depths, all he can perceive is a suffocating cloak of darkness. "Where are you?" he shouts into the void. His words echo in the silence, accompanied only by the sound of his flailing arms in the water. Suddenly, a seam of bright red appears in front of him, opening to reveal the burning red eyes that have haunted him since the first sighting.

Thomas heard a haunting voice calling out to him, urging him to come closer. Frustrated and unnerved, Thomas demanded to know why the voice wouldn't leave him alone. The voice grew more insistent, promising to make the torment stop if Thomas would only heed its call. Thomas, feeling a surge of anger rather than fear, challenged the unseen presence, declaring that he was not afraid of something he had ensnared in his net. The creature, sensing Thomas's growing fury, taunted him, asking why it did not instill fear in him. Suddenly, Thomas stopped swimming and defiantly proclaimed that there was no reason to fear something he had captured. The creature's response triggered an overwhelming surge of pressure in Thomas's head, causing him to fear that he might pass out. The voice continued to coax Thomas, promising an end to the unsettling dreams and the mounting pressure in his head, even offering to spare his town and his wife, Mary. Enraged by the mention of his wife,

Thomas lashed out at the unseen entity, inciting its fury in return. The dream culminated in a deafening roar as Thomas jolted awake, screaming and clutching his head in terror.

Tumbling out of bed in a panic, his screams piercing the silence of the night. The pounding in his head made it feel as if it might burst, until his wife Mary reached out and held him close, her touch seeming to alleviate the pressure. As he gradually calmed down, Thomas confided in Mary about the worsening nightmares that plagued him. Mary reassured him, reminding him about the upcoming town hall meeting where they hoped to find a solution to the menacing creature that had appeared on their shore.

Although Thomas was dreading the meeting and the difficult questions he knew he would face, his father's advice to remain a strong leader for the town echoed in his mind. Despite his inner turmoil, Thomas agreed to return to bed, seeking solace in Mary's embrace. While Mary drifted back to sleep, Thomas remained awake, consumed by his anxieties for the rest of the night.

6

Thomas and Mary walked into city hall and were met with a scene of emotional turmoil. The room was packed with townspeople, some shouting in anger and others sobbing in grief. Thomas observed heart-wrenching scenes of fatherless children sitting quietly next to their now-widowed mothers, some trying to console their mothers while others attempted to stay strong for their younger siblings. The weight of the tragedy was palpable, and Thomas couldn't help but dwell on the vibrant lives the men had led before the incident. Amidst the somber atmosphere, Thomas and Mary located James and his wife, who ushered them to sit with them as the mayor prepared to address the gathering from the podium.

"Hello, everyone. This is a somber morning, but I thank you all for being here. We are confronted with an unknown threat at our border, and I urge you all to remain indoors until we can establish contact with the government." The crowd erupted with questions and concerns. People demanded to know why the government had not been contacted sooner. One woman passionately suggested that the men should have been prevented from leaving, while another pointed an accusing finger at Thomas, insisting that his warnings should have been heeded. Then, the situation took a turn for the worse.

The next person to stand up was Johnathan's wife. Her eyes were red as she walked over to Thomas and said, "Why didn't you do more to stop them?" Her words triggered more outbursts from others in the room. Some blamed Thomas for starting his season early, claiming that it led to the early departure of the captains. Mary attempted to calm the situation, but Thomas abruptly stood up and left the room. James, now standing, shouted over everyone, "How dare you all! That boy showed your loved ones the footage of what happened and gave his warning. Thomas is a hero; he saved my life and the lives of some crew members in the room." Crew members from the Northern Star voiced their agreement. "Instead of blaming Thomas, you should look at the ones who are actually in charge and who could have made a difference," James stated before leaving to follow after Thomas. The room fell silent, with only Mary crying into James's wife's arms.

James stepped outside and spotted Thomas perched on a bench, gazing at the snow-covered ground. Approaching him, James was about to speak when Thomas preempted him, saying, "I could have done more." Tears began to well in Thomas's eyes, falling onto the snow beneath him. Taking a seat beside him, James reassured him, "You fulfilled your duty as a captain and brought your crew home. Never forget that, Thomas." Despite James's words, Thomas still seemed burdened. "I wish things had turned out differently, James. If only they had listened,"

Thomas lamented. Placing a comforting hand on Thomas's back, James replied, "They are at peace now and free from nightmares." Thomas's head shot up as he asked, "Wait, have you been having nightmares?" James hesitated before admitting, "Some of the crew and survivors have been haunted by nightmares of that creature." Thomas sat up, his eyes searching James's. "Has the monster been reaching out to you?" he inquired. James nodded, confirming that it had. "So you're saying we've all been having nightmares, and the creature is communicating with you?" Thomas questioned, incredulous. James shook his head, finding it hard to believe.

Just as they were about to delve into further discussion, Thomas' phone suddenly rang. He glanced at the caller ID and saw that it was Zoey from the hospital. "Hello," Thomas answered. "Thomas, you need to come to the hospital right away. The men you rescued have finally regained consciousness."

7

Thomas and James hurriedly made their way to the hospital, where chaos reigned. Nurses darted around, wheeling IV bags and attending to patients, while doctors hastily flipped through charts as they rushed to various rooms. Family member's faces, etched with worry, crowded the entrance, desperately seeking news about the survivors of the recent attack.

"How are we going to find Zoey in all this madness?" Thomas questioned, scanning the frantic scene. Just then, a small tug at his shirt drew his attention, and he turned to see Zoey, her expression intense and focused. "Follow me and stay close," she instructed, her urgency palpable.

They trailed closely behind her until they reached a quieter hallway, a temporary oasis amidst the hospital's turmoil. "This is where we're keeping them," Zoey said, her voice steady but tinged with underlying tension. "One patient is still undergoing tests, but the other is awake in his room."

Suddenly, Thomas halted her. "Wait, why are you not informing the mayor or the police first?" he asked, concern knitting his brow. Zoey let out a deep sigh, the weight of her words evident. "My husband didn't make it back. He was on Jonathan's ship as a new deckhand. He didn't tell me he was going because he knew I would oppose it. He hoped to help me with my student loans."

As a tear slipped down her cheek, she paused, gathering her thoughts. "I don't blame him or Jonathan. My anger is directed at the Mayor. He should have intervened but chose not to. They should have listened to you, Thomas. I don't trust the police right now, but I trust you both. You might be able to uncover the truth from him, and I believe you'll share it with the people."

Thomas, feeling a surge of sympathy, expressed his condolences but pressed on. "But why do you think the people in lab coats would know anything?"

Zoey took a deep breath, her resolve hardening. "His name is Jacob Zimmerman. When I looked him up, I discovered he's a government researcher, a paleontologist who studies dinosaurs. And honestly, that creature we saw sure resembled something straight out of Jurassic Park."

Exchanging concerned glances, Thomas and James steeled themselves before continuing to follow Zoey, each step bringing them closer to the truth hidden within the hospital's walls.

Zoey pushed open the door to a dimly lit room where an Indian man lay in bed, struggling to spoon pudding into his mouth. "Oh, hello! Can I assist you with something?" he asked, looking somewhat startled. Thomas stepped forward, his demeanor serious as he introduced himself. "I'm Thomas Harris, Mr. Zimmerman, and this is James. We need to ask you a few questions."

Zimmerman's expression shifted to one of apprehension as he instinctively reached for the alarm button beside him. However, James moved quickly, intercepting him and taking away the device. Anger flared in Thomas as he settled onto the edge of the bed, his gaze piercing. "You're going to tell us what you know about that thing outside before I have to make things unpleasant for you."

Zimmerman raised his hands defensively, a tremor of fear in his voice as he uttered, "You won't believe me." Thomas narrowed the distance between them, his expression challenging. "Try me," he replied. The anxiety in Zimmerman's eyes deepened as he confessed, "All right, I'll tell you the truth. I work for the United States government. My research lab was stationed in the remote stretches of the Pacific, conducting groundbreaking studies on how to resurrect dinosaurs. We discovered Plesiosaur DNA embedded in kelp on the ocean floor. We collected samples with plans to clone them back to life, but then things took an unexpected turn.

As my team initiated the tests, something else emerged that wasn't a Plesiosaur. We decided to proceed with cloning it at its infant stage, but when it came to life, it kept growing far beyond our expectations. From my phone, I witnessed the chaos unfold as our base erupted in a fiery explosion, propelling me into the ocean.

For seven harrowing days, we drifted helplessly on a makeshift raft, constantly aware of that unseen monster lurking just below the surface. It felt as if the creature needed us close. Whenever we attempted to swim to safety, it would draw us back as if it were toying with us. Then, out of nowhere, we noticed your boat in the distance. But as we approached, an unbearable pressure built in our heads, and we lost consciousness. That's all I remember, I swear."

James hesitated, stepping back as he regarded Thomas with concern. "You really don't think?" he asked, his voice tinged with uncertainty. Thomas, visibly agitated, stomped his feet in frustration. "It used them as bait to lure us in," he retorted, his eyes narrowing with conviction. With a deep breath, he straightened himself and approached the window, his gaze fixed on something distant beyond the glass. "You mentioned you work for the government. Are they actually going to come and fix this mess?" Thomas inquired, a mix of hope and skepticism in his tone.

Zimmerman reclined on his bed, his tone nonchalant as he announced, "Our contract clearly states that if anything goes awry, the government will sever all ties. I'm afraid you're on your own."

Thomas, feeling a surge of frustration, pivoted sharply and grabbed his phone from his pocket. With an unwavering determination in his voice, he handed it to Zoey. "No, we're not done here," he insisted, his eyes gleaming with resolve. "You're going to recount every word you just shared with me. We'll record it and attach our video to it. Then we'll blast it out across all social media channels."

Zoey began recording, and Zimmerman shouted, "Don't do this! The government will show up and..." Thomas slammed his fist on the nightstand and said, "Let them come; I'll introduce them to the beast on my doorstep."

ACT 4

THE SHADOW OF FEAR

1

All Thomas could see was an oppressive darkness that enveloped him like a thick fog. He raised his hand in front of his face, but it vanished into the void. The silence was deafening until a voice emerged from the shadows, echoing ominously around him. **"How long will you bear this pain?"** it asked, its tone hauntingly familiar.

"This could all end if you just come to me."

Thomas, feeling a surge of defiance, replied resolutely, "No."

"Ah, you are strong," the voice taunted, growing more sinister. *"But you can't stop me. I will be here forever. Just come to me, and I will go away."* The insistence in its tone intensified, reverberating in his ears.

"Why me? Why do you want me?" Thomas questioned, desperation creeping into his voice.

The response was chilling as if the voice was brushing against his very soul. *"Because of what you did to me."*

A shiver coursed down his spine, raising the hairs on the back of his neck. Suddenly, he heard a clicking hiss behind him, making him whirl around. There, in the suffocating darkness, were the burning red eyes that had haunted him since the day they first met.

"You will come to me, Thomas," it hissed, ***"or maybe Mary will."***

With that, Thomas jolted awake, gasping for breath, his surroundings slowly coming into focus. He was still in bed, and Mary was peacefully asleep next to him. He lay back down, his heart still racing, and turned his gaze toward the window. Snowflakes danced gracefully outside, their delicate patterns contrasting sharply with the turmoil in his mind. Sleep eluded him, leaving him wide awake in the stillness of the night.

2

Thomas stepped into Kodiak Bar & Grill, the familiar sound of clinking glasses and the low murmur of conversation greeting him. The dim lighting cast a warm glow over the faces of patrons, many with worry etched deep into their features as they sought solace at the bottom of their drinks. Scanning the room, he finally spotted

James perched at the bar, deep in conversation with Brain.

Making his way over, Thomas slid onto a bar stool, the leather cool against his skin. He gestured to Brain, who stood behind the bar and asked for a glass of water. Just as he received it, a concerned voice broke through the noise.

"You still having nightmares?" James inquired, concern flickering in his eyes.

Thomas stared at the glass, its surface rippling slightly in the dim light, lost in thought for a moment before responding. "The nightmares are getting worse. That thing is trying to get me to... to do it," he confessed, his voice barely above a whisper, heavy with unease.

James took a sip of his coffee, the bitter aroma mingling with the scent of fried food in the air. "Same for me, too. It wants me to set sail," he said, his brow furrowed as he glanced around, almost as if the very words might summon their shared dread.

The silence that settled felt thick and suffocating until Brain broke it, his voice steady but laced with urgency. "Your video has made the news, but the government is doing everything it can to keep a lid on it. I've been getting phone calls from people asking about that thing out there."

Thomas's grip tightened around the glass, the coolness a faint comfort against the rising tide of his fears.

"I've been receiving calls too," Thomas said, a frown creasing his brow. "But for some inexplicable reason, all flights to and from Alaska have been canceled. It seems we're truly on our own."

Brain, his hands busy cleaning a dusty glass, looked up, concern etched on his face. "What are you planning to do, Thomas?"

Taken aback, Thomas furrowed his brows. "Why are you asking me?"

Setting down the glass with a soft thud, Brain leaned closer. "No one trusts that Mayor. You're the only one who managed to escape that monster lurking outside. The town believes in you, Thomas. So I ask again—what's your plan?"

Thomas inhaled deeply, the weight of responsibility pressing down on him. Memories of his father's words floated to the surface, echoing in his mind. He had always dreaded this burden; he never wanted to lead. Yet, something shifted within him. "Thomas, the men who don't want to lead are the ones everyone follows," his father had said, the wisdom now resonating profoundly. As the realization washed over him, he finally understood the truth behind those words.

Thomas rose from his chair, his posture commanding attention in the dimly lit room. "James," he declared, his voice steady and authoritative, "gather every man in town for a meeting here tomorrow morning. I want to see all of them, without exception. And make sure the Mayor knows he's invited as well."

James, ever the diligent aide, nodded with a knowing smile. "Of course, Captain."

As Thomas began to stride toward the door, a sharp voice interrupted him. "Thomas, what are you planning to do?" Brian called out, concern etched on his face.

Thomas paused, turning back slightly, a mysterious glint in his eyes. "Nothing... yet," he replied, leaving an air of intrigue lingering in the room.

3

Thomas stood on the swaying deck of the Northern Star, his gaze fixed on the turbulent sky, which roiled with dark, angry clouds. The heavy winds whipped against his face, chilling him to the bone, while the monstrous waves surged higher and higher, crashing against the hull with a thunderous roar. Doubt gnawed at him—was it wise to set sail in such treacherous conditions?

"Set sail, Thomas. You've been in worse. Come and see me," a haunting voice called out from the depths, slicing through the howling wind. He leaned over the railing, peering into the churning waters below, knowing full well what lurked beneath the surface. "I won't come to you, not yet, but soon," he replied firmly, his heart racing.

"No, now, Thomas! I don't want to wait!" the voice grew louder, more insistent, driving a shiver down his spine. He turned away, feeling an unsettling shift in the air as if the very creature he feared was displeased. Suddenly, a ripple splashed behind him, and Thomas froze, slowly turning back to face the water.

Emerging from the abyss above him was the creature—a nightmarish form hovering ominously. Its body, scarred and ancient, resembled tough, weathered leather, glistening in the feeble light. The head was an unsettling blend of dragon and serpent, crowned with sharp, menacing horns that jutted out like weapons. Its long, sinuous tongue flicked out, tasting the air as it drew nearer. Yet, despite the terror looming before him, Thomas stood resolute, unyielding to fear.

"I'll be seeing you soon," he declared defiantly. With a terrifying roar, the monster reared back its head and slammed down towards him.

Startled awake, Thomas found himself in the familiar confines of his bedroom, his phone ringing insistently beside him. Heart pounding, he quickly composed himself and answered it. It was James, his voice urgent, instructing him to get to the dock immediately.

After hanging up, Thomas hastily threw on his coat, stirring Mary from her slumber. "What's going on?" she asked, her voice thick with sleep and concern.

"I don't know, but something urgent is happening at the dock," he replied, slipping on his boots. She watched him with worried eyes and urged, "Be careful."

"I will," Thomas assured her, but the weight of uncertainty pressed heavily on him as he raced out of the house, ready to confront whatever awaited him.

4

Thomas deftly maneuvered his car to a halt at the edge of the bustling dock, the salty breeze tousling his hair as he stepped out. The scene before him was chaotic; bright blue police lights sliced through the dusk, illuminating officers as they restrained several sailors, their faces a mix of confusion and fear.

His heart raced as he scanned the crowd, finally spotting James amidst the turmoil. Without a second thought, Thomas sprinted toward him, urgency propelling his steps. "What's going on?" he shouted, breathless and alarmed.

"Everyone's eager to set sail; their nightmares have gripped them," James replied, his voice heavy with concern.

Panic surged through Thomas as he witnessed the escalating situation. He began shouting, desperately urging the sailors to halt their frenzied attempts at escape, hoping to quell the storm brewing around them.

"If you set sail, you're doing exactly what it wants," Thomas declared, his voice rising above the clamor of the crowd. The police officers nearby exchanged worried glances, one of them responding, "We can't stop them; there are too many." Undeterred, Thomas kept shouting, his frustration boiling over. He lunged forward, gripping the shoulders of several men to hold them in place, determined to make his point. Just then, the deep roar of a boat engine cut through the air.

Thomas and James stood at the edge of the dock, their eyes squinting through the thickening fog as a small boat glided silently toward the mist. In the dim light, Thomas recognized the solitary figure on board—Chris Johnson. Panic surged within him, and he sprinted to the end of the dock, his voice breaking the stillness as he shouted, "Chris! What are you doing? Stop!"

Chris turned to look back, his eyes filled with a deep sorrow that pierced through the haze. "I just want it to stop, Thomas," he replied, his voice raw with emotion. Tears streamed down his cheeks, glistening like jewels against the backdrop of gray. "I'm sorry, Captain," he whispered, the weight of his words hanging heavily in the air.

As the boat neared the precipice of the dense fog, an eerie silence enveloped the dock. Suddenly, the monstrous silhouette emerged, its piercing red eyes glowing ominously against the dark canvas of the night sky. All movement ceased as onlookers stood frozen, captivated by the unsettling sight. The creature's cavernous mouth opened wide, revealing a long, dark red tongue that slithered down, glistening under the faint light. With an almost serpentine grace, it wrapped around the boat, lifting it effortlessly off the water and launching it skyward, leaving gasps of disbelief in its wake.

The monster let out a bone-chilling roar, its massive head crashing into the boat with a force that sent waves rippling across the water. Panic-stricken screams erupted from the crew, echoing across the darkening sky, but those watching from the dock remained frozen in shock, wide-eyed and breathless. Thomas stood rooted in place, his chest heaving as he tried to absorb the chaos unfolding before him. As the creature finally pulled back, its fierce red eyes locked onto Thomas, piercing through the mist that enveloped it. In that haunting moment, the beast vanished into the swirling fog, leaving an eerie silence hanging in the air.

Thomas felt a surge of emotion as a flood of memories of Chris washed over him. He vividly recalled the day they first met, a sunny afternoon when he was just ten years old. His father had introduced Chris as the new cook, and the warmth of that moment still lingered in his heart. Now, however, Chris was nothing more than a bittersweet memory.

James spoke to him, but Thomas was lost in his thoughts until he felt a reassuring hand on his shoulder. "We need to go, Thomas," James said, his voice steady but urgent.

Thomas glanced around and noticed that everyone was frozen in place, paralyzed by fear. His gaze wandered to the towering lighthouse in the distance, its silhouette stark against the dimming sky.

"Get everyone home, James," Thomas instructed, determination rising within him. "And still tell them we're meeting later. There's someone I need to talk to." His voice was firm, echoing with the weight of unresolved emotions as he readied himself for the task ahead.

5

Thomas navigated the winding road leading to Kodiak Point Lighthouse, the salty air filling his lungs as he drove. As he parked his car, the sun dipped low on the horizon, casting a warm golden glow over the rugged landscape. He stepped out, feeling the cool breeze brush against his skin, and gazed over the hill where a thick blanket of fog hung just above the water, shrouding everything in an eerie, ghostly hush. Though the creature remained unseen, an unsettling certainty gripped him—he knew it lurked somewhere in the mist.

With determination, Thomas approached the creaky old door of the lighthouse and raised his hand to knock. The sound echoed softly in the stillness. Moments later, the door swung open to reveal Philip, his eyes alive with urgency. "I was waiting for you to get here. Come inside," he said, gesturing for Thomas to enter. Without hesitation, Thomas stepped across the threshold, the air inside thick with anticipation.

Thomas settled into the creaky chair, its worn surface a reminder of countless conversations held in this small, dimly lit room. He glanced towards the back, waiting for Philip to emerge from the shadows of the back room. "You said you were waiting for me. Why?" Thomas inquired, curiosity tinged with impatience.

A voice echoed from behind the door, fervent and intense. "Because I now know what that thing is!"

Puzzlement spread across Thomas's face as he tried to process the urgency in Philip's tone. Finally, the door creaked open, and Philip stepped into view, clutching a well-worn Bible with an air of grim determination. He flipped it open and thrust it towards Thomas, revealing a page adorned with a crude drawing of the creature that had instilled fear in the hearts of everyone who had witnessed it.

"What is this?" Thomas asked, rising to his feet, his heart racing as he examined the illustration of the terrifying monster.

Philip sank into a nearby chair, his expression serious. "That thing out there is no dinosaur, no mere relic from a bygone era that those men in lab coats thought they resurrected. No, they've unleashed something far older—something that predated the very creation of man itself. It's a Leviathan."

Stunned, Thomas sat back down, the weight of Philip's words crashing down on him. He had heard whispers of the Leviathan, a colossal creature conjured by God that commanded the very forces of nature. "Philip, are you sure?" he asked, skepticism lacing his voice.

Philip pointed towards the window, where ominous clouds swirled, dark and heavy. "What else could it be? No dinosaur could haunt your dreams or summon a storm like that."

Though doubt flickered in Thomas's mind, he found it hard to dismiss Philip's assertion entirely. "I came up here for advice, so... how did the Leviathan die?" he asked, an uneasy feeling settling in his stomach.

Philip shrugged, his shoulders heavy with the weight of uncertainty. "There's nothing definitive about what happened to the Leviathan—only the stories that have surfaced over time. The truth is lost in the layers of myth."

Thomas let out a deep, weary sigh, the weight of the situation pressing down on him. "Well, that's certainly helpful," he murmured, his gaze darting nervously out the window as if searching for answers in the swirling clouds.

Philip, still focused on Thomas, leaned forward with an intensity in his eyes. "So what's the plan?" he pressed, eager for direction.

Drawing in a steadying breath, Thomas turned back toward his friend, determination flickering in his eyes. "We take the fight to it. There's no other way," he declared, the resolve in his voice cutting through the uncertainty.

Nodding thoughtfully, Philip rose from his chair, the hardwood floor creaking beneath him. He crossed the room to a well-worn desk nestled in the corner and opened a drawer that had seen better days. With a clink of metal, he retrieved a set of gleaming keys.

"If you're going to face that thing, then you'll need a ship," Philip said, his voice steady as he handed the keys to Thomas. "These are the keys to the USS Resolute, the battleship currently on display at the museum."

Taken aback, Thomas stepped back slightly, a flicker of hesitation crossing his features. "But that ship belongs to your family; I can't take that," he objected, a hint of guilt threading through his words.

Philip waved off his concerns dismissively, a flicker of pride sparking in his gaze. "My grandfather, Thaddeus Blackwood, commanded that ship against invaders during the war. You need something with cannons to confront that monster. I'm certain my grandfather would be proud to see you honor his legacy by sailing her."

Overwhelmed and at a loss for words, Thomas felt a surge of hope. This was exactly what he needed—a fighting chance against the looming threat that haunted his thoughts. "Philip, I promise I won't let your grandfather down," he vowed, sincerity echoing in his tone.

With a gentle, supportive hug, Philip stepped back, a fierce determination in his eyes. "Give that monster what for," he encouraged with a grin.

A smile broke through Thomas's anxious demeanor as he strode toward the door, the keys clutched tightly in his hand, ready to face whatever awaited him.

6

Thomas navigated his car down the winding road to Kodiak Point Bar & Grill. As he approached, he noticed a restless crowd of men huddled together outside, their expressions a mix of concern and anticipation.

After parking, he stepped out into the crisp air, instantly sensing the weight of the collective gaze bearing down on him—dock workers, sailors, policemen, and every other man in Kodiak Point had turned their attention to him. With determined strides, he made his way to the forefront of the gathering, where James awaited him.

"They are all waiting, Thomas," James said, his voice steady but laced with urgency.

Thomas surveyed the sea of worried faces, each etched with anxiety and uncertainty. He felt an overwhelming pressure settle on his shoulders as he tried to gather his thoughts. Words eluded him, swirling in his mind like leaves tossed by a storm. After a moment of hesitation, he took a deep breath and began to speak, hoping to reassure them all.

"Most of you recognize me, and many of you are familiar with my father. I grew up in this town, just like so many of you. But today is not like the others; today, we find ourselves standing at the edge of the unknown, facing a monstrous threat that has been lost to the sands of time, now rearing its terrifying head in our midst. This creature has invaded our nights, weaving nightmares that have compelled our loved ones to act in ways we couldn't have imagined. It has taken from us more than we ever dared to think we could lose, but it hasn't stripped us of everything.

I understand your fears — they resonate in the silence that blankets us, a heavy shroud of anxiety. No one is coming to rescue us, a truth that weighs heavily on our hearts. You might consider fleeing, but what would that truly achieve? You asked me to develop a plan, and I am prepared to share it. Today, we will face our deepest fears head-on, reclaiming the power that has been stripped from us.

I envision waking up tomorrow, sunlight spilling into my room, casting a warm glow that dances across the sheets and softly illuminates my wife's peaceful face beside me. I yearn for that moment, reveling in the thought of countless days ahead when we can cherish each other and build a wealth of memories.

Philip has entrusted me with the keys to the USS Resolute, a magnificent battleship bristling with cannons, ready to unleash our defiance. I understand that I am asking a great deal from each of you, but this is the path we must take. I swear to you, as I pledge to my crew, that by dawn tomorrow, each of you will be safe in the arms of those you love.

So now, I turn to you: who among you stands with me?"

As silence enveloped the air, delicate snowflakes drifted softly down, blanketing the crowd in a serene white. Yet, in an instant, the stillness shattered as voices erupted in unison, echoing through the frosty air. "Yes!" they shouted, their breath forming clouds, each declaration thick with camaraderie and resolve. Sailors grasped each other's shoulders, their faces illuminated with determination, embodying brotherhood in the face of looming peril.

Thomas stood momentarily stunned, caught off guard by the passionate response. Leaning closer, James murmured with a knowing smile, "That's how you lead men." Grateful for the insight, Thomas nodded appreciatively before raising his voice, directing everyone to head home and warn their families to stay indoors. "Let's reconvene at the museum!" he commanded, his tone steady and firm. The men immediately set off, the urgency evident in their hurried steps as they raced to deliver the message of caution.

Turning back to James, Thomas asked, curiosity lacing his words, "What happened to the Mayor? I thought he would be here to intervene." With a raised eyebrow, James replied, "Apparently, the Mayor and all his belongings vanished from his home, along with his car."

Thomas shook his head, exasperation surfacing in his expression. "Worthless till the end," he muttered. "I'll meet you at the museum. I need to make a phone call."

James gave him a supportive pat on the shoulder. "I'll see you over there," he said with encouragement.

With a small smile, Thomas took out his phone, his fingers trembling slightly as he attempted to call Mary.

7

Thomas leaned against his car, the cold metal pressing into his back as he held his breath, waiting for Mary's response. The weight of the evening's revelations hung heavy in the air. He had just disclosed everything—what had transpired at the docks, the startling truths revealed at Philip's, and the ominous plans that lay ahead.

"Why does it have to be you, Thomas?" Mary's voice erupted through the phone, raw with emotion.

"It has to be me, Mary. I'm the only one who can do this," he replied, his voice filled with determination, but the line fell silent, thick with tension.

Before he could gather his thoughts, Mary's voice broke the silence again, tinged with frustration and hurt. "Even when we were kids, it was always you. Everyone looked up to you, followed your lead, and you always shied away from the spotlight. And now you're facing a monster straight out of the Bible, and still, you insist it has to be you? But what about me, Thomas? I'm your wife, and I don't want to become your widow."

Gazing up at the gray sky, his heart ached at her words. Snowflakes drifted down, swirling gently in the air, reminding him of how he felt when they first met in the first grade. He had fallen for her then, and that love had only deepened over the years.

"Mary, I'm doing this for you," Thomas said, his voice softening. "I've never met anyone who challenges me like you do. Every day with you inspires me to push my limits. If I don't lead these men, how will I ever face you if something goes wrong? I need to protect the light you bring to my soul every single day."

He could hear her quiet sobs on the other end, and his heart sank. "Please, don't make promises you can't keep," she whispered, her voice trembling.

Thomas took a deep breath, determination surging through him. "Now you know me, Mary. I always keep my promises."

With a heavy heart, he hung up, feeling the chill of the wind against his skin. He turned his gaze back to the ocean, where the fog swirled ominously, and storm clouds gathered above like a foreboding shroud.

Nodding to himself, he climbed back into his car, the engine rumbling to life as he steered toward the museum, the weight of his love for Mary pressing him onward into the looming darkness.

8

Thomas stepped onto the grounds of the Kodiak Whale Tour & Fisherman Museum, where the salty air mingled with the scent of the ocean. The open-air museum was a vibrant tapestry of maritime history, showcasing an impressive array of artifacts from sailors' adventures over the decades. Crowning the exhibit was the majestic USS Resolute, a colossal dreadnought that loomed overhead. Its formidable silhouette was marked by towering cannons, armored plating that spoke of past battles, and the intricate machinery of its steam turbine engines. The sight of this imposing vessel was nothing short of breathtaking, embodying the spirit of exploration and adventure that Thomas and his companions had come in search of.

Thomas stood on the weathered dock, scrutinizing the worn hull of the boat before him, when he heard a voice break the silence. "So this is what you want to take out to sea?" Turning, he found himself face to face with Timothy Daiz.

Timothy glanced over the vessel, his brow furrowing as he added, "This boat is a beauty, but it's riddled with problems." The sunlight glistened off the old wood, revealing the years of neglect it had endured.

Intrigued, Thomas stepped closer, his curiosity piqued. "Can it sail?" he asked, hope creeping into his voice.

A knowing smile crept across Timothy's face. "Yeah, with some work, I'll have it ready by the end of this week," he replied, gesturing toward the various tools strewn about, hinting at a long, busy road ahead.

But determination was etched on Thomas's face as he turned to Timothy.

"Did you not hear me earlier? We are doing this today." His eyes shimmered with anticipation, envisioning the open sea.

Shaking his head, Timothy sighed, a flicker of disbelief crossing his features. "It's a hundred-year-old ship. Do you think I can have it ready by today? Do you realize how much manpower that will take?" The weight of reality settled between them, the sound of waves lapping at the shore echoing the urgency in Thomas's heart.

"Well, it's a good thing we showed up just in time!" James shouted, his voice echoing across the open field. Thomas and Timothy turned to see six hundred men standing tall, clutching an array of tools in their hands, their faces set with fierce determination. The sun glinted off the metallic surfaces, creating a shimmering effect amidst the crowd.

Thomas couldn't help but smile as he glanced at Timothy. "Is that enough, men?" he asked, a hint of doubt in his voice. Timothy, however, responded with a wicked grin that spread across his face. "Oh, that's more than enough," he replied, confidence radiating from him.

Taking a deep breath to steady himself, Thomas felt a wave of relief wash over him. "Alright, men! Let's get started," he declared, his voice ringing out with authority as he rallied the troops, ready to embark on their daunting task ahead.

ACT 5

THE HUNT BEGINS

1

Repairs on the battered ship were in full swing, with Timothy at the forefront, coordinating efforts to ensure they would be battle-ready. Above deck, the atmosphere was tense as a crucial meeting unfolded on the bridge. Thomas sat across from James and Samuel Reed. They were joined by Adam Hernandez, a well-built Hispanic man with the presence of a natural leader, who served as the captain of the Kodiak Point police. Alongside him sat Henry Jackson, a grey-haired army veteran with deep lines etched into his face, the result of years spent in service.

"We have enough ammunition onboard to face that creature without any issues," Henry stated robustly, his voice steady. "But we can't afford to be the first ones attacked."

James nodded thoughtfully, leaning forward. "We need a distraction, something to keep the monster occupied while we approach from behind."

Henry agreed, his eyes narrowing in contemplation. Adam interjected, "What about a decoy ship?"

Samuel shook his head vigorously. "All the ships were destroyed; we don't have anything left to use."

Then, Thomas spoke up, his voice cutting through the tension. "Not all of them are gone. My ship can still sail." The room fell silent, each of them weighing the implications of his words.

Henry nodded solemnly, his brow furrowed with concern. "Then we have a chance," he said, the weight of the situation heavy in the air. "But the next question is... who will sail? Whoever takes on that role will be risking their life."

James, leaning against the wall with a furrowed brow, spoke up. "I can set the Northern Star to autopilot, but... no. That monster will sense it. Someone needs to be on the boat, and that person is me." His voice was firm, cutting through the tension as the room fell into an uneasy silence.

Thomas replied, "There's no way I'm letting you do that." He stepped forward, his features set in a mix of resolve and protectiveness.

James smiled, a glint of defiance in his gaze. "Sorry, Captain, but I'm disobeying your orders. You all need to focus on getting everything ready. I'll keep that monster busy while you get into position." His voice was steady, but the underlying tension was palpable.

Thomas, frustrated and boiling over, stomped his foot on the creaking wooden floor. "You're not doing this," he asserted, his voice echoing in the now hushed room.

"Everyone, give us a moment," Thomas commanded, his tone leaving no room for argument. Samuel, Adam, and Henry exchanged worried glances before stepping out, leaving just Thomas and James in the dimly lit space, the weight of their impending choices hanging heavily between them.

"What are you thinking? I'm not letting you do this," Thomas said.

James stepped closer and replied,

"Thomas, you may be my captain, but I'm still your uncle. My brother would be furious if I allowed you to go through with this. You still have a life to live, and I'm nearing the end of mine. I'm making this decision, and you can't stop me."

Thomas, wiping tears from his face, said, "What about your daughters, your wife, my auntie? You would really put them through this?" James closed his eyes and said, "I'm doing this for them, Thomas. I can't let this plan fail. You must lead these men. But in the chance things go sideways, Make that future son-in-law of mine the first mate. He will do great."

James hugged Thomas, but Thomas was too busy trying to hold back his tears to embrace him in return. "It was an honor to sail with you, Thomas," James said as he left the room. Overcome with emotion, Thomas fell to his knees and pounded the ground as the man he regarded as a second father walked out the door.

2

As James strode down the corridor, a heavy silence enveloped him. Men paused in their tasks, their eyes fixed on him, their expressions a mixture of sorrow and admiration. Confusion washed over James as he continued walking, more and more faces turning to meet his gaze. Unable to ignore the weight of their stares, he came to a halt and called out, "What's the matter with you men? Get back to work."

Paul stepped forward, his expression serious yet respectful. "Samuel told us your plan," he said, his voice steady. "The men just want to show you our respect. We know you weren't our captain, but we still look to you as our leader."

A smile spread across James's face as he placed a reassuring hand on Paul's shoulder. "You better give my little girl the world, young man. That's my last order to you." Paul bowed his head, a sense of gravity in his voice as he replied, "Yes, sir."

"Good men," James said with pride, and as he resumed walking, he couldn't help but notice how every man had momentarily paused their duties to acknowledge him.

Once he disembarked from the ship and made his way through the museum's spacious halls, a sudden sound broke the stillness behind him. He turned to find a sea of men on the deck, their hands coming together in thunderous applause, their cheers echoing like a wave crashing against the shore. Looking up to the bridge, he caught sight of Thomas, giving him a solemn nod of respect.

Unable to contain the emotion swelling within him, James turned away, the warmth of unshed tears stinging his eyes. As he walked away, the resounding cheers of the men lingered in the air, a powerful reminder of their camaraderie and support.

James stood on the main deck of the Northern Star, the cool mist of the thick fog swirling around him. He gazed into the shrouded waters, aware of the mysteries that lay beyond the veil, but his mind was too full of memories to dwell on them. As he walked the weathered deck, he let the scent of salt and aged wood envelop him, each grain of the deck whispering tales of the years he had spent aboard this vessel.

The crew members he had the honor of leading flickered through his mind like shadows—a gallery of faces, each tied to a shared adventure. He could almost hear the echoes of their laughter and camaraderie, forming a tapestry of stories he cherished and recounted to his daughters when he returned home.

He recalled the day he and his brother, Trent, had stumbled upon this boat—once a hunk of junk with peeling paint and a crooked mast. James had practically laughed in disbelief as he stood beside his brother, surveying their ambitious purchase. "Trent, you can't be serious! You really want to buy this boat?" he exclaimed, disbelief etched across his face.

Trent walked confidently along the deck, brushing his fingers against the weather-beaten railings. "This is where our journey begins, brother. One day, we'll set sail, and people will witness what we can accomplish."

James joined him at the bow, both of them staring out at the endless horizon that promised adventure. "Trent, you're going to be a father soon. Do you really think it's wise to take on the role of captain right now?"

Trent chuckled, a sound that mingled with the wind as it whistled past them.

"I'm doing this for my son. He will take the helm one day and carry on what we started here today."

A smile crept onto James's face, though a hint of amusement danced in his eyes. "You fool! Lydia is only three weeks pregnant—you don't even know if you're having a son!"

But Trent merely laughed again, the joy in his voice unmistakable. "He's going to be a boy, and I'm going to name him after our father—Thomas. He'll be a better captain than I am, mark my words."

James smirked, "I wish I could see into the future like you, brother." Their laughter had faded into the ether of memory, leaving behind a warmth that lingered even as he returned to the present.

Suddenly, his phone buzzed insistently in his pocket, snapping him back to reality. Glancing at the screen, he saw a message notifying him that they were ready. James tucked the phone away and made his way toward the bridge, a sense of purpose propelling him forward.

He slid his hands over the polished wheel of the Northern Star, the familiar touch grounding him. As he engaged the vessel to leave port, he felt a rush of anticipation course through him. Peering into the fog ahead, he whispered to the boat, "Alright, girl, one last ride."

4

James expertly navigates the North-ern Star into the thickening fog, the eerie silence enveloping him. As he pierces through the dense mist, a furious storm suddenly erupts around him. Streaks of lightning illuminate the dark sky, momentarily revealing the chaos of crashing waves and whipping winds. Thunder roars like a wild beast, echoing in his ears as he strains to see through the relentless sheets of rain.

His heart races as he finally spots what he has been yearning for—a pair of glowing red eyes piercing through the darkness, watching him with an intense, unyielding gaze. A surge of adrenaline courses through him; he knows he has arrived at his destination.

With trembling hands, James slows the vessel to a halt, allowing it to rise and fall with the tempestuous sea. He takes a deep breath, the salty spray mixing with the rain on his face, before donning his raincoat. Determinedly, he makes his way down to the main deck, ready to confront whatever awaits him in this stormy night.

James trudged across the weather-beaten deck, the relentless rain lashing against him like a thousand icy needles. The wind howled ferociously, threatening to uproot him, but he held his ground, maintaining a steely composure. As he reached the bow of the ship, he peered into the depths of the stormy night, his heart racing in anticipation of the monstrous creature he knew lurked just beyond the shadows.

Suddenly, two fiery red eyes flickered open before him, igniting the darkness and illuminating the hulking figure of the beast. The creature's gaze pierced

James to his very core, an electrifying connection that sent shivers down his spine. Yet, he stood resolute, his expression unyielding in the face of terror.

The beast reared its massive head, showcasing a grotesque body, sinewy and powerful. It opened its gaping maw, revealing a long, sinuous tongue that flicked out like a serpent, tasting the air. James remained steadfast, his voice steady as he proclaimed, "I was once afraid of you, a specter that haunted my dreams and nearly extinguished my faith. But now, as I stand here, I feel a strange sense of satisfaction."

Just as the beast let out a thunderous roar, a blinding explosion erupted close to its head, sending shockwaves through the air and momentarily shattering the tension between the two.

Loud cannon fire reverberated through the air, each blast painting the night sky with bursts of fiery illumination. James stood frozen, momentarily in shock, as the colossal beast continued to take hit after hit, showing no sign of slowing down. In the distance, the USS Resolute emerged, drawing closer with a thunderous rhythm of cannon fire that sent plumes of smoke spiraling into the night.

On the deck, men scurried about in a frenzy, grabbing flares to launch into the sky as the monstrous creature struggled to regain its bearings, completely overwhelmed by the assault. Behind him, James heard footsteps approaching rapidly. He turned to see Samuel and the rest of the Coast Guard boarding, clad in sleek wetsuits, ready for action.

"What are you doing here?" James called out, a mix of confusion and urgency in his voice.

Samuel stepped forward, a determined look on his face. "Captain's orders," he replied, handing James a walkie-talkie with a firm grip.

James clicked it on, his heart racing. "Hello?" he said, his voice steady despite the chaos surrounding him.

Thomas's voice crackled through the speaker, laced with intensity. "When I became captain, I made a promise that all my crewmates would make it home safely, and that includes you!" The weight of those words hit James like a tidal wave of emotion, and he couldn't help but smile through the uncertainty.

"Yes, Captain," he responded, a renewed sense of determination filling his spirit as he prepared to face the looming threat.

Back on the bridge of the USS Resolute, Thomas gripped the radio tightly, his voice steady yet urgent as he commanded his crew to keep loading the massive cannons. The sound of metal clanging against metal echoed around him, a reminder of the relentless pace required for their survival. He focused on the ship's wheel, steering the vessel directly toward the colossal Leviathan that loomed ahead. The atmosphere crackled with tension as Thomas locked eyes with the creature, the same fiery red orbs that had haunted his dreams now staring back at him, filled with a fierce and primal intensity. The weight of their impending clash hung heavy in the air, a moment of fate spiraling closer with each tick of the clock.

5

Thomas stood at the helm, his voice commanding above the cacophony of whistling flares and booming cannons. The ship rocked beneath him, but he kept a steady hand on the wheel, eyes fixed intently on the monstrous Leviathan looming in the turbulent waters. "Don't let it submerge!" he barked at his crew, urgency etched on his face.

The beast thrashed and writhed, desperate to escape the relentless barrage of cannon fire, but each shot found its mark, preventing it from diving below the waves. Meanwhile, James and the Coast Guards were in full action, launching flares into the darkening sky and casting nets into the churning sea, determined to ensnare the creature before it could slip away.

As the battle raged on around him, Thomas urged his crew with fervor. "Pour it on!" he shouted, his adrenaline surging. Suddenly, the Leviathan reared its enormous head, unleashing a bone-cracking roar that reverberated through the air. The sound was so powerful that everyone on deck staggered back, hands clasped over their ears in a futile attempt to block out the cacophony.

At that moment, the sky lit up as bolts of lightning rained down around the ship, blinding Thomas with searing brilliance. He shielded his eyes, the world around him transforming into a tempest of sound and fury as they continued their battle against the creature of legend.

Thomas Vison returned to the chaos, realizing too late the error of his judgment in getting too close to the Leviathan. The monstrous creature loomed ominously, its massive jaws poised to strike. As he scrambled to his feet to regain control of the boat, it was already too late; the bear-like behemoth crashed its massive jaw into the vessel, sending the crew sprawling and screaming in panic. The relentless force of the Leviathan was overpowering, crushing the hull under its weight.

In the midst of the panic, Thomas instinctively sprang into action. Without a moment's hesitation, he seized a spear and bolted onto the deck, where chaos reigned. The frantic crew's terrified faces turned toward him, their shouts urging him to retreat. But Thomas's mind was made up; he felt a fierce determination surge through him.

With rage igniting his spirit and re-solve etched across his features, he locked his gaze onto the colossal beast. Heart pounding in his chest, Thomas leaped, landing squarely on the gaping maw of the Leviathan. Focusing all his strength, he drove the spear deep into the creature's flesh, unleashing a wave of newfound fury that coursed through him. In that moment, he transformed from a mere man into a warrior, con-fronting the monstrous adversary with courage that defied all odds.

The Leviathan released its grip on the ship, sending Thomas sprawling back onto the deck. Distracted by the chaos, he quickly regained his footing and shouted into his radio, "Fire!"

A cacophony erupted as cannons boomed, flares streaked through the night, and harpoons launched into the darkness, all while the monster unleashed a resonant roar that echoed across the water. The air was thick with smoke, illuminated by the vibrant red of the flares colliding with the beast.

As Thomas strained to see through the haze, he noticed the piercing red glow of the Leviathan's eyes begin to fade to a lifeless grey. Its massive head fell backward, and its colossal body floated eerily to the surface, marked by gaping wounds from the relentless cannon fire.

A hush fell over the crew as they watched the sight unfold. Sensing the shift in the battle's tide, Thomas raised his hand and commanded, "Stop!" The chaos around him paused, the collective breath held, waiting for the fate of the fallen beast.

Thomas made his way to the bow of the ship, eager to witness the aftermath of their battle. The massive form of the Leviathan lay motionless in the shimmering water, its eyes wide open yet devoid of life—the vibrant glow that once radiated from them had vanished completely.

With a deep breath, Thomas picked up the radio and spoke, his voice steady but filled with emotion. "We won."

A thunderous roar of jubilation erupted from the crew, reverberating through the air as cheers and cries of triumph mingled together in a triumphant symphony. The tempest that had once raged around them began to recede, its ferocity waning alongside the thick fog that had shrouded their victory.

As the storm dissipated, everyone gathered on deck, their eyes fixed on the horizon. The morning sun broke through the clouds, casting golden rays that painted the sky and glistened on the water's surface, warming their souls.

Thomas sat down on the edge of the ship, relief flooding over him. He felt a profound sense of fulfillment; he had kept his promise, and now, with the dawn breaking before them, he knew that everyone—every single person—would soon be heading home.

6

Thomas stood on the weathered dock, his gaze fixed on the Leviathan's massive form being hoisted onto the shore by towering cranes. The sound of metal clanging against metal echoed in the brisk air. As he contemplated the sight, James approached, his boots thudding softly against the wooden planks.

"So, what happened to the plan?" James asked, his brow furrowed with curiosity.

Thomas sighed, a hint of apprehension in his voice. "I fear my auntie more than going against my uncle's wishes."

James chuckled, the sound lightening the tension. "Good choice! Thank you for saving me, Thomas."

A smile crept across Thomas's face as he nodded, momentarily forgetting their troubles. "What do we do now?" he inquired, the uncertainty lingering in the air.

"We rebuild and get ready to set sail," James replied, determination gleaming in his eyes.

Thomas raised an eyebrow, his confusion evident. "You really think the crew wants to set sail right now?"

James's expression brightened, and he responded, "We are fishermen, Thomas. It's what we know best. Besides, this little town is about to become quite popular."

Thomas turned to him, intrigued. "What do you mean?"

Stepping forward, James's enthusiasm bubbled over. "The crew uploaded the footage of the battle online, and apparently, it's garnering a ton of views...whatever that means. People are swarming here, eager to interview us and learn about what happened."

Shock washed over Thomas as he processed the news. "Okay, but how is all that attention going to help us? We're about to turn into a tourist trap," he remarked, a hint of frustration creeping into his voice.

James nodded slowly but added, "Yes, but with that attention comes potential sponsors. More money means better equipment. More people here could mean more business for everyone. We just have to ensure we have a mayor who can keep it all in order."

Thomas burst into laughter. "I never thought I'd see you in politics," he teased.

James looked momentarily perplexed. "Wait, not me. Someone else needs to step up."

Thomas raised a hand, cutting him off gently. "Sorry, James, but the people want you to take over. As of today, you are officially retired from the Northern Star, per the captain's orders."

For a moment, James stood stunned, his eyes downcast. Then, a smile broke across his face, and he nodded. "Yes, captain."

Together, they stood, side by side, gazing out at the endless horizon where the blue sky kissed the shimmering sea. Thomas broke the silence, a sense of hope in his voice. "I'm happy to see the open blue sky again."

ABOUT THE AUTHOR

Atticus Blackwood is a talented author hailing from Athens, GA, whose literary works seamlessly blend the genres of realistic fiction, mystery, and supernatural elements, creating a captivating and unique reading experience. His stories transport both young adult and adult readers to immersive worlds that skillfully merge the ordinary with the extraordinary, weaving together suspense and intrigue. Atticus is known for his writing style, which effortlessly combines a casual and approachable tone with expert storytelling prowess, allowing readers to deeply connect with his well-crafted characters and enthralling narratives. Fueled by a deep-seated passion for creating compelling adventures, Atticus has the remarkable ability to transform everyday moments into extraordinary tales that continue to resonate with readers long after they've finished reading.

www.ingramcontent.com/pod-product-compliance
Lightning Source LLC
Chambersburg PA
CBHW071241300726
48975CB00002B/504